Jagua Nana's Daughter

**A sequel to
Jagua Nana**

Cyprian Ekwensi

Spectrum Books Limited
Ibadan
Abuja • Benin City • Kaduna • Lagos • Owerri

Published by
Spectrum Books Limited
Spectrum House
Ring Road
PMB 5612
Ibadan, Nigeria

in association with
Safari Books (Export) Limited
1st Floor
17 Bond Street
St. Helier
Jersey JE2 3NP
Channel Islands
United Kingdom

Europe and USA Distributor
African Books Collective Ltd.
The Jam Factory
27 Park End Street
Oxford OX1, 1HU, UK

Reprinted in Nigeria 1989, 1993, 1995, 2000

ISBN 9-7824604-35

Dedication

To Joop, Olu, Yinka, Oyinkan, Gbenro and all
my friends at Spectrum

Contents

Chapter One

The Mirage

The lecture was over, and so was the cocktail party.
As the band struck the first chords of the Nigerian
National Anthem, the chatter subsided to a whisper.
The multi-costumed, multi-national guests, many of
them still carrying cocktail glasses in their hands,
froze wherever they were on the lawns of the Institute
of International Affairs and tried their best to hold an
attention position with the alcohol still glowing in
their veins.

Listening to the Police Band render the Nigerian
National Anthem, Liza Nene noted with pride the
richer and more dignified sound. As soon as the
anthem ended, small talk resumed.

'Let's go now,' Saka Jojo whispered in her ear. He
tightened his grip on her long slim fingers. 'Let's
move before the rush.'

Liza smiled and gave him a sideways glance.

Saka held Liza by the curve of her hips and guided
her through the crowd. Liza flowed with the crowd,
Saka behind her. He never failed to be delighted by
her tall rangy figure, the lissom limbs and the
quickness of movement.

The Cameroons Ambassador and his wife stood
beaming as group after group passed before them and
greeted them. The Ambassador's wife wore a crown
gele, flamboyant and colourful in the shape of a

Boeing 747. As she nodded and shook hands, the headtie split the air with subsonic sounds.

'Let's get nearer,' Saka said, 'and shake hands with the Ambassador.'

'Patience!' Liza said. 'Let them finish their greeting...don't you see? That looks like a special group.'

'It was a good lecture,' someone behind them was saying. 'I learnt quite a lot.'

'What was the title?'

'Something about BORDER CLASHES AND TERRITORIAL INTEGRITY...something like that...'

The lecture had drawn this large audience to the Institute because of public interest in the recent border clashes between Nigeria and her neighbours, especially Cameroon and Chad. One such clash had led to the burning and looting of border villages on both sides. The newspapers had reported the death of fishermen and soldiers alike from Nigeria and the Cameroons, and the presence of white mercenaries.

'The Cameroon Embassy were clever to organise the lecture. It helped me understand things better.'

Saka said to Liza, 'You're in court tomorrow?'

'Oh dear,' Liza sighed. 'Don't remind me...'

'Those your court cases *never* end.' Saka was teasing. 'Adjournment after adjournment. That's why no sensible businessman ever takes his problems to court, *if* he can help it. But I suppose you Lawyers have to eat...'

Liza allowed the remark to float. She knew when she was being needled and how Saka felt about the Court, the lawyers and the whole judicial system in

2

Nigeria. To him most High Courts were courts of in-justice and nothing could change his opinion. Liza had always tried to explain to him that he was wrong, but he never listened.

'My dear, justice delayed is justice denied,' Saka rubbed in.

The air was still and humid, and stars twinkled in the night sky.

They stood a little away from a group gathered before the Cameroon Ambassador.

Whispers went round that the group now exchanging greetings with His Excellency the Ambassador was made up of Cameroonians resident in Lagos.

While the Cameroons residents bowed and scraped before the Ambassador and his wife, Liza was watching them closely. Suddenly, in the midst of that motley crowd she noticed a woman of extraordinary personality and beauty towering above the rest of them. Something about her seemed familiar.

Liza felt momentarily breathless as the woman's image became fuzzy. This was a mirage, she told herself, a trick of the light. As she watched with interest, the image of the woman standing there seemed to dissolve. Could that be Kate Nene her one-time step-mother whom everyone at Jos knew as Auntie Kate — here among the Lagos social set? Impossible. As a child she was told that her father had died in Greece. Liza had been content to believe that Kate was her mother until gradually the truth came out.

Even as she strained to get a better view and as if by telepathy, the lady herself turned her head towards

Liza's direction and their eyes met across the sea of
heads. A wave of recognition shot between the two
women and Liza found herself trembling.

'God above!'

'What's up?' Saka asked. Liza felt eagle eyes
piercing her face.

'Nothing — I just feel faint.' Liza's hand moved
towards the nearest chair which was placed near
some flower beds.

Saka stood over her. 'You look . . . like you've seen
a ghost!'

'I have,' Liza said. 'Over there!'

Pictures of her childhood days drifted across her
mind. She saw the rocks and hills of Jos . . . *She saw
herself aged three or four, playing with her doll before the fire
one cold night in the harmattan. Auntie Kate, away as usual
with her white lovers from the tin mines. The doll fell into
the fire. Liza trying to retrieve it, her own clothes catching
fire. Screams. But for sister Heide rushing in from outside
and beating out the fire . . .* The dizziness passed. Liza
rose to her feet.

'Did you notice that woman?'

'I don't follow . . .' Saka's look of confusion was not
feigned.

'Auntie Kate . . . Kate Nene . . . Kate Nene
Papadopoulus . . .

'Saka, that's my father's concubine.'

'Your father, what are you talking about?'

'I've never told you this, Saka. My father lived at
Jos Plateau. He was Greek . . .'

'No wonder'

'A tin miner. And that woman there — that bitch,
deceived him and said she was my mother.'

4

'What!' Saka did not know he had raised his voice. But when he saw the looks on the faces of the guests he checked himself.

'I have never told you this Saka, because it didn't matter. *I am the daughter of a famous woman called JAGUA NANA. I have never met her and today I am a Barrister and Solicitor of the Supreme Court of Nigeria by the Grace of God.*'

'Tell me!'

Again Saka Jojo was almost shouting, 'Does it matter? But why hide the truth from me?'

'That's why I want to find out. I could kill that woman for her hypocrisy.' Liza clenched her fists. 'The bitch! The infertile bitch!'

'Keep your voice down!' Saka tried to hold her back, but Liza shook his hands off.

'Look at her, still selling herself at her age. See the young whiteman beside her.' Indeed Auntie Kate had hooked her hands with a tall white escort in a light grey safari suit. Saka held Liza in check.

'Control yourself.'

Liza clenched her fist.

She took three swift strides forward, but Saka quickly pulled her back, 'Where to now?'

'I want to confront her.'

'I said calm yourself... Not here! You cannot catch up with her in this confusion.'

The stream of guests had stopped flowing. Liza noticed that Auntie Kate was whispering to her white escort and glancing over her shoulder with frightened eyes.

By the time Saka had shaken hands with the Cameroons Ambassador and his wife, the queenly

Auntie Kate and her escort had slipped away. Liza dragged Saka with her, and just as they gained the street she saw Auntie Kate get into a Peugot 504 beside the whiteman at the wheel, bang the door shut as the car sped off.

Near the Honda Prelude parked in the same street, Liza stopped to regain her breath. She fumbled in her bag, turned and glared at Saka.

'I should have confronted her,' she was trembling with rage.

'Liza, I've never seen you so upset . . . Listen I came in the BMW . . . leave your own car here . . . I'll drive you home. One of my drivers can deliver your car safely to your place later. I can't trust you driving to Surulere in this mood.'

'No, Saka . . . I want to go home. It's late, and I have a case tomorrow in the High Court, remember?'

'Don't worry,' Saka said. 'Your case will be adjourned on some technicality . . .'

'How do you know?'

'It always happens.'

'You speak like a disgruntled business man.'

'Surely you mean an international tycoon, Chairman and Managing Director of Saka Jojo Nigeria Limited, Group of Companies' he said smiling. 'Liza, listen to me . . . don't drive that car in this mood . . . Come home with me, you can go to court from my own home in the morning . . .'

Liza shook her head. 'And abandon my two young children, only to have your wives carve me up for breakfast?'

She saw the hurt look in his eyes. Saka was the

macho man she admired, a man who had built up for himself a play-boy image.

He squeezed her wrist with affection. 'You can always have the guest-room.'

'Aha! The advantage of being the mistress of a tycoon ... and you deceive yourself, Chief Saka Jojo, that in this our Lagos your three wives, three *official* I mean. You deceive yourself that your wives do not know of your numerous mistresses! One day it will happen ... I'm sure they know my name, where I live, everything. As long as I'm out of sight, its okay. Bringing your mistress to the house is another matter!'

He started. 'Liza!'

But she went on, 'The great Chief Saka Jojo, a connoisseur of women, wine and fashion, one of the *nouveau riche* who struck oil money ...'

'Enough! ... the press boys may be around.'

Liza began to laugh. Chief Saka smiled too.

'Are you coming with me or are you not, Liza? I am tired and my body needs you.'

'No, thank you, Saka. I want to go home to Ngozi and Obi.'

'But your maid is there — or has she left you?'

'Maid is one thing, Mummy is another.'

'What of Daddy and Uncle? ... If I remember rightly, your maid is efficient, and the school is just around the corner from where you live ...'

'You're impossible when you want something.'

'I don't want just something ... I want my woman ...'

'You know too much about my affairs, Saka ...'

'You are my mistress and when I'm on heat I think

better... Listen to me! Forget Auntie Kate! Let bygones be bygones. The wounds will heal. After all, what does she matter to you now? Whether she likes it or not you've made it!'

'But I still don't know my mother! And that's why I came back to Nigeria. To find my mother. Can't you see? And Auntie Kate is the link. She could lead me to my mother!'

She slipped beneath the wheel of the Honda. An instant later, the engine exploded into life and began to purr. Saka Jojo instinctively stepped back, out of the way. Liza handled the car with ease and guided it out of the parking lot, putting the puzzled face of Saka Jojo out of her mind.

'Auntie Kate in Lagos'... Liza kept murmuring to herself. 'And who was the white man with her? Trust her to pick a whiteman lover or husband any day. She has a complex. She must be much older than that man. But why did I not see her when I could have given it to her? Maybe she saw me first and was dodging, the bitch'.

Liza drove towards Surulere in the suburbs of Lagos, and down a small lane off Alhaji Masha Street, parking in the small compound of one of the medium income houses built in the days when Governments talked less and achieved more with limited resources. The lucky buyers of houses in those days bought cheap and then transformed the houses into prestigious homes.

The three-bedroom bungalow in front was occupied by the Landlord, a retired civil servant named Alabi. His children were all abroad in Universities, studying medicine, engineering and

8

law. He lived with his wife whom Liza had seen only about three times since she moved in.

Liza had reshaped the annexe at the back into the comfortable flat that she now occupied and it was here that she made her way, after parking the Honda and securing it for the night against the marauding car snatchers of the city.

Liza pressed the bell several times before she heard the shuffling footsteps of the maid.

'Who's that?' came the frightened voice from within.

'Open the door, Titi.'

'Madam, are you back?' The voice came faintly through the locked door but there was relief in it. The unbolting of several locks and the shifting of bars followed.

At last the door swung back. 'Welcome, Ma.'

'Were you sleeping?' Liza asked.

'No, Ma. I'm inside waitin' for your return.'

Liza threw her handbag on the love-seat in the sitting-room and immediately, Titi picked it up and walked ahead with it into the bedroom and placed it on the dresser.

'You need anything, Ma? What about chop?'

'Nothing, Titi. Are the children asleep?'

'Yes, Ma.'

Liza began taking off her jewellery. 'Anybody ask of me?'

'No, Ma ... Goodnight, Ma.'

Liza checked to see how the children lay. A feeling of satisfaction descended on her. She vowed to do everything she could to give them that mother-love she herself had missed. She tucked the cloth carefully under the girl Ngozi who was long limbed, a **carbon** copy of herself. The boy Obi could always control his limbs when asleep.

In the bathroom, she turned on the hot water and began to undress. Her eyes wandered briefly to the reflection of herself in the full-length mirror. Critically she examined her arms, her tummy and her behind for traces of fat. The flatness of her belly belied the fact that she had produced two children. Her jutting and shapely rump was the provocation that drew the males, especially when she put on jeans and high heels. That trace of Greek blood gave her a rich and breath-taking complexion that was African and Mediterranean at the same time.

Having bathed in the slightly hot water mixed with pine disinfectant and bath salts, she drained away the fatigue and the day's frustrations with the bath water. As she sat before the mirror, combing out her hair and placing it in curlers, she thought about Auntie Kate. Was it a mirage? Finally she slipped into the soft cotton nightgown and climbed into bed. She opened 'Criminal Procedure', leafed through it, then remembered to set the alarm for six o'clock.

She must have dozed off before she heard the door-bell. She glanced at the bedside clock. It was already 1.55 a.m. She waited and listened. The bell rang again. She tiptoed to the door. Security had become a new instinct in the cruel city of Lagos. Life and limb were the playthings of pistol-and-matchet-carrying intruders who turned every night into a nightmare.

'Open, it's me, Saka . . .'

'Do you know the time? It's two in the morning!'

'I wanted to make sure you got home safely.'

She opened the iron burglar proof, then unchained the main door. Saka came in, bringing with him a puddle of water.

'Raining, is it?'

'Drizzling... You mean you didn't know?'

'The air-con' didn't let me.'

'You always turn it on too high...

He pushed past her and walked possessively into the bedroom.

'There's no one there, lover!'

'I wasn't expecting to find anyone, but just to make sure.'

'And if you did? I'm not your *wife*... Three wives should be enough to satisfy any sex maniac.' She locked the door, went back to the bedroom, while he helped himself to food and drink from the fridge.

'It's not everywhere I can go at 12 midnight and feel free to eat.'

She made a face at him. 'You millionaires are always targets for poisoned coffee, heart attack and high BP! I don't envy you.'

He paid no attention. He was munching from a plate of cold salad and helping himself straight from the half-bottle of chilled *mateus rose*.

'Those wives of yours with their fat bottoms. Don't they cook for you, or all they do is just...'

'Enough now, Liz! None of your business... And if I ever hear you mention...' He rolled her over and smacked her bottom. 'Yours is not all that small after all. Only more shapely.'

When he had satisfied his hunger, he began removing his shoes. 'You locked the door I hope?'

'I believe so.'

Now he was fully undressed. He took a cloth from the drawer and smelled its cotton smell.

'Saka, my love, what did you tell your wives?'

'No more of that!' His eyes wore a glazed look. He reached out for her and snuggled against her. After a while he lifted his lips from her breast and said, 'A dog with food in its mouth does not bark.'

'Meaning?'

He pulled her nearer and she submitted freely. He took her passionately and insatiably, again and again, with the same uncontrolled hunger he had shown over his food.

At one point when he cried out, she scratched his face. 'Quiet. You'll wake the children!'

'I just went mad, when I remembered how you looked at the party...'

She must have drifted into heavy slumber for when the alarm began to ring and she reached out to turn it off, she found that she was alone.

The nursemaid said, 'The hot water is ready for bath, Madam.'

'Where are the children?'

'Ready for school, Ma. They're eating breakfast.'

'Good morning, Mummy!' sang two happy voices, and their faces appeared in the doorway.

The High Court premises began to fill with men and women litigants, their relations and friends, and soon, with black-robed solicitors. One famous lawyer was struggling with a heavy suitcase full of tomes. He had built up a reputation for fighting oppressed people's causes. For this reason the Nigerian Security Organisation often invited him for 'chats' and he had responded by building a seven-foot wall topped with spikes round his Chambers and securing his residence behind barrier after barrier of ironwork.

His cases attracted press attention and already the press box was full with young men and women standing by notebooks and tape recorders, ready to file their reports and to interview him specially, afterwards.

'Let me help you with that, Senior...' Liza reached out for his heavy suitcase.

He laughed. 'Thank you, learned Counsel, I can manage.' Two boys in open-necked shirts ran towards the Senior Advocate and relieved him of the suitcase.

They moved ahead of him into court number five and began slowly to off-load the fat volumes and to ensure that the flagged pages were all in place.

The judge had still not arrived, and Liza was standing within the court premises with a group of State Defence Lawyers when she saw the silver Porsche 924 drive in.

The door opened and Saka stepped out and began walking toward her. He waved a greeting to the standing group of lawyers, as Liza excused herself and followed him to the foot of the tall and shady Indian Almond tree.

'I hope you've recovered now ... I have to leave for Amsterdam this morning.'

'What's up?'

'Business,' he said. 'A telex message from our trading partners was on my desk as I got into the office.'

Liza said. 'Your frequent international jetting is no

longer news . . . get me something nice, a necklace, some perfume . . . When do you return?'

'A few days, no more. That's if I don't move to Geneva.' He smiled. 'Take care, Liz . . . By the way I began some inquiries at the Cameroons Embassy, trying to trace your Auntie Kate.'

'Any luck?'

'Not yet. But I left someone on the job. It may not be all that difficult because of her white escort. His name is Alberto Ricardo, a construction engineer.'

Liza felt the excitement rising in her. 'So that's it! Auntie Kate has not changed. My father was a tin miner at Jos Plateau and she was his mistress. She will always go for the professional expatriates. If only I can trace her! She holds the key to my mother's whereabouts.'

'I don't mind your tracing her. It's the confrontation I don't like . . . She deceived the world and got away with it . . . That's over now.'

Saka Jojo, resplendent in his suit, stretched out his hand and patted her shoulder. 'Just take care, whatever you do. I have already spread the word. If you can only be patient.'

'Safe journey,' she said.

Liza rejoined the group, but everyone was now moving to the Court room, for the whisper spread that the judge was already in Chambers.

'Cou—uuurrrt . . .'

The judge entered the Court, bowed, was bowed to, and sat down. The chairs, benches, rumbled as the court sat down.

Liza's case was listed fifth, behind two land cases, one murder case, and the case of unlawful detention

14

filed by the brilliant lawyer.

The brilliant lawyer was on his feet still citing one authority after the other to buttress his argument when about three hours later, the judge yawned and called for an adjournment. 'There's no power supply. The fans are not working and it's too hot,' he grumbled.

'Will learned Counsels please take dates?'

Liza joined the learned counsels from opposing sides congregated round the register, carrying diaries.

Liza said to herself, 'Saka was right; adjournment after adjournment.' This time it was for another eight weeks. Liza rose, bowed to the Court, and with heavy tomes under her arm, walked into the fresh air, thinking, *Auntie Kate could become a mirage.*

Chapter Two

The Mother

Jagua Nana had been living in Ogabu since the death of Uncle Taiwo, when news reached her that Rosa, her one-time friend and room-mate in Gunle, had come back to her village in the East, a dozen kilometres from Ogabu.

'My good frien' Rosa,' Jagua beamed, remembering the days when they had tramped the streets together in Lagos. 'I mus' go and see her.'

Turning to her mother who was busy cooking, she told her all about Rosa. 'Ah wonder whether she return final, or she just come see home people. As for me, ah done tire for village life!'

She set out early one morning and, true enough, found Rosa in her village, but to Jagua's surprise, she saw Rosa nursing a new-born infant with surprising maternal love.

'What, Rosa! . . . Which time you born dis pickin'?'

'Three month now,' Rosa smiled. She was looking more rosy now. Her skin had an unusual glow. Jagua recognised the bleaching-cream colour which was becoming so fashionable these days. Portions of her face showed the deep burns from excessive use of the cream.

'Congratulations,' Jagua said. She pulled a small stool towards her and sat near Rosa who was busy with baby things — napkins, talcum powder, feeding bottles.

'Way de Papa of de pickin'?' Jagua asked.

'He go work. He will return for evening. I tink you know David? We marry after all.'

Jagua remembered the young man in a blazer who was always hanging around them.

'Am glad for you.'

Rosa measured Jagua with a careful look. 'How you dey, since all dis time?'

'Ah stay for village, with my mother,' Jagua said, 'You know that my Papa die.'

'Ah hear the news.'

'Nex' Sunday will make one year,' Jagua informed her. She took the infant from Rosa and cooed at it lovingly.

The touch of the tender baby-skin stirred in her that loneliness that had been with her since she began to live in the village. She saw now that the grief over her dead child Nnochi, had killed her spirit, weakened her will and isolated her from life. What had happened to that *Jagua* whom the men fought over, with whom Chief Ofubara of Krinameh had been so infatuated? The Jagua who had driven the bandit Dennis Odoma to commit daring robberies to win her favour, and made Uncle Taiwo a political partner?

Jagua gave the child a loving smile and handed her back to her mother. Then, as if rocked by a sudden pain she rose to go, blinking back the tears.

Rosa said in a surprised tone, 'What happen? You never stay wit me, and you wan' go back like dat? Anyting?'

'Noting.' Her voice had deepened into a sob.

'Why you act like say someting' happen?'

18

Jagua turned away so that Rosa, who was smaller and more petite than she was, came round to see her face.

'Stay now,' Rosa pleaded. 'Make we talk and chop. We get plenty story to tell, Jagua. Ah go tell you about Lagos since you lef' de *Tropicana* Night Club. Ah go tell you how everyting' change, till money no dey for town. Dem done broke down de Club!'

Jagua was not listening. She stood still for a moment, then gathered herself together. 'I jus' remember someting' . . . Nex' Sunday, we will hol' Memorial Service for Papa . . . You go come help me prepare chop? Try an' come for Saturday afternoon . . . Den we fit talk about everytin'. You fit sleep for my place . . . for morning, we go go Church togedder. You can bring you pickin'.' A note of pleading had come into Jagua's voice.

Rosa smiled and said, 'When David return, ah will beg him to allow me.'

Rosa saw Jagua off and Jagua watched her till she turned the corner of the footpath and disappeared behind the trees. Now she felt the pain of the aborted pregnancies, and remembered with regret how fertile she had once been.

After her reckless life in Lagos and the sober life in Ogabu, Jagua Nana re-examined her life. She asked herself how a woman could be complete without one man she can call her own, and no child that she herself had produced.

The thought of Chief Ofubara of Krinameh came to her. Of all the options available to her, returning to Krinameh seemed to be the most compelling. To go back to Lagos was out of the question.

In the crowded bus on her way back from visiting Rosa, Jagua Nana decided to go back to Krinameh, to Chief Ofubara. His invitation was still valid.

On Sunday morning, Jagua Nana rose early, but her mother had been up before her, and Mama's friends and relations were already busy cooking, sweeping, washing and making other preparations for the memorial service of Jagua Nana's late father.

A bus stopped on the road in front of their house, and Jagua saw Brother Fonso get down. She rushed outside to welcome him. Brother Fonso and his children trooped across the courtyard, accompanied by a strange woman.

'Sister,' he said, embracing her.

'Welcome,' said Jagua Nana, speaking in Igbo. 'We received the things you sent for the feast... How's Onitsha market?'

'Good' he said.

Jagua was surprised and pleased. She least expected that Brother Fonso, an Onitsha market trader, would spare the time to be present. Not only that, to arrive in good time, with his wife and children, and this matronly-looking woman whom Jagua now remembered.

'Sister Heide,' she said, 'How you manage?' She noticed that Sister Heide did not look a day older. Still the same housewifely type, quietly dressed, self-effacing.

Brother Fonso told Jagua Nana that he would explain about Sister Heide in full later. He settled his family in the living room and went with Jagua to the

kitchen where Rosa was busy checking the heavy pots
of rice and stew.

'Brother, this is my frien' Rosa . . . She came from
her village to help me.'

Rosa gave her usual rosy smile. 'Welcome, Brother
Fonso. I remember you, when you come visit Jagua in
Gunle. Long time now.'

'Yes, yes! . . .' Brother Fonso recalled.

Rosa's eyes examined his face. 'Welcome.'

Jagua Nana took Fonso aside.

'I am planning to make a small donation today on
behalf of the family to bring honour to Papa's
memory.'

Brother Fonso looked at Jagua Nana and his eyes
darkened. 'It's good.'

Jagua said, 'You know that Uncle Taiwo, the late
politician left some money . . . I'm giving part of it to
the church. I already gave some to the people of
Krinameh.'

'Good, sister. God will replace!'

They walked back to the house. Again, Jagua
wanted to know how Brother Fonso came about
bringing Sister Heide to this function.

'Be patient . . .'

But Jagua could not hold back the
memories . . . *Sister Heide and Auntie Kate, room-mates,
living just across the street from them . . . the white tin miner
who came only at weekends in a pick-up van to take Auntie
Kate to the hills . . . the Bauchi Light Railway train to Zaria
which came in punctually most nights . . . Auntie Kate,
always impeccable and glamorous in the steps of Alice Faye
of Hollywood . . .*

The church bell rang and they hurriedly got

together their prayer books and set off for the service.

Jagua mumbled a prayer for the repose of the soul of her late father. The priest read the lesson. He told them that Jagua's father David Obi had taken the gospel deep into Eastern Nigeria at a time when oracle worship defied Christianity. That as a true evangelist, Jagua Nana's father had tried to bring up all his children to respect the word of God. The priest prayed that his daughter Jagua Nana and his other descendants should continue to follow his noble example and put their fate in the hands of God.

Then he announced that the Obi family had donated six hundred pounds towards the construction of the new place of worship, already in progress.

The service ended.

They all met outside the church and exchanged greetings and pleasantries before returning to the Obi family residence for refreshments.

In the small living room, Brother Fonso said prayers and again praised the memory of their late Father who had devoted his life to spreading the word of God.

Jagua went and sat beside Sister Heide.

She said, 'Mama, how now?'

'Am well, Jagua Nana, you don become *Madam*. Small gel of yesterday.'

'Na so. Every small gel must become Madam one day.'

Sister Heide was silent. Jagua was silent. The room was silent, save for the tinkling of spoons and knives on china plates, as the guests ate.

To break the silence, Jagua spoke almost in a

whisper so that only Sister Heide could hear her. 'Since my pickin' die, ah never born anodder pickin'.'

Sister Heide said, 'Your pickin'? The one you born for Jos? Way you leave with Auntie Kate?' She laughed. 'Who say de pickin' die?' She snorted. 'Your pickin' no die.'

'What?'

'I say your pickin no die.'

Jagua Nana watched Sister Heide's face for signs. She could read nothing but a dead seriousness.

Brother Fonso interrupted them. 'Jagua, come and serve drinks to everybody,' and Jagua went with him, still shocked.

After the party, Fonso and his family with Sister Heide beside them, gathered to leave. The bus that had brought them arrived from Owerri enroute Onitsha.

Most of the guests going that way trooped in and made off, with much hand-waving and nose-wiping.

'Ah will come to Onitsha sometime,' Jagua said to Brother Fonso as the bus rolled off.

Jagua boarded a lorry bound for Port Harcourt. She was bent on reaching Krinameh the same day. The lorry arrived at Port Harcourt in the evening, and Jagua against all advice, managed to catch the last of the waiting dug-out canoes for Krinameh. She paid her fare and took a seat in the gently rocking boat. A male passenger in a robe gave Jagua a strong familiar stare as though he would speak, but decided otherwise.

Jagua recalled her first visit to Krinameh some

years ago. Freddie Namme was then lusting after the teenage Nancy Oll while she — Jagua, tortured herself for him. Young Nancy had little to offer but firm breasts and an athletic body. She knew nothing about life, and could not guide a man through its turbulence.

And the result? They returned from England with two children born by Nancy, Freddie plunged into politics without knowing what it was all about, and he was murdered in cold blood. To this day, as she sat in that boat bound for Krinameh, Jagua Nana still had troubled dreams about Freddie Namme and how he could have avoided being brutally killed.

The boat grounded at Krinameh beach in the waning light. Jagua inquired about Chief Ofubara from a young man who was standing beside a basket full of shrimps and crabs.

'Try there!' the young man pointed.

As Jagua walked towards the palace, she noticed a strange excitement, almost a commotion ahead of her. Children stopped their play, pointed at her and ran ahead towards the palace. A young man with an Afro haircut came up to Jagua.

'Are you not Jagua Nana?' he asked.

'Das me.'

'My father, Chief Ofubara always talks about you. I was very small when you first came here. You won't remember me.' The young man took her bag from her and together they walked towards the palace. 'Jagua don come-O!' cried a woman who was suckling a baby. She ran before them with the news. The palace was all clamour and bustle as they entered and greeted. In the wonder of the chatter and

24

noise, Chief Ofubara came into the sitting room in slippers. Jagua curtesied in greeting, but instead Chief Ofubara walked quickly towards her and embraced her. His cloth slipped and Jagua had to put it back in place to avoid his being unduly exposed.

'Welcome, welcome! So you got my message at last.'

'Message? I no get any message. Ah just come because ah promise to return.'

'So many messages! So many.' Chief Ofubara began issuing instructions. 'Tamuno! ...Tamuno! ...'

A young and elegant girl in her teens came into the room. 'Jagua, this is my junior wife, Tamuno!' She gave Jagua a hostile look.

Jagua greeted her. Somehow she reminded Jagua Nana of Nancy and Jagua disliked her with that instinct of a deadly rival.

'Tamuno, this is my wife Jagua — from Ogabu. I already married her. I paid her dowry, but she ran away back to her place...'

'Ah done return,' laughed Jagua.

'Go prepare her room for her — quick now! Abi you dey sleep?' Chief Ofubara could not conceal his pleasure.

The girl wiggled past him and he slapped her on her behind. She threw a coquetish glance at the Chief and Jagua Nana read the message that she was the current favourite wife.

That night Jagua gave him the excitement he had nearly forgotten. Slowly undressing, baring her body in little portions, while he waited hungrily, she tantalised him in the half light of a candle.

'God! You Jagua, you no dey grow o!',' said Chief

Ofubara gazing wide-eyed at the glowing skin, the flat tummy, and when she returned to hang her clothes over the back of a chair, the perfectly proportioned and shapely hips of the original Jagua. This was not a woman before whom any male could be impotent. She still mumbled obscenities and when he took her in his arms, she surrendered herself with glazed, half-shut eyes and hungry lips.

She came out of the trance to sip a neat glass of home-distilled gin and to say goodbye to the world, amidst the scented pillowcases and silken sheets.

Chief Ofubara seemed to have dozed off when a knock sounded at the door. Tanumo peered into the room.

The Chief lifted his head angrily. 'What is it now?'

'Chief, ah still dey wait you.'

'What for?' asked Chief Ofubara.

'Not mah turn to sleep wit you dis night?'

'Oh my God!' cried Chief Ofubara, 'so you no see say ah get big stranger?'

Hands on hips, jutting out her young bosom, Tamuno fairly screamed at him. 'You drive me because you see Jagua woman. Not de same ting?'

'No,' said Chief Ofubara. 'Dis one different. Dis one be original Jagua woman.'

'Ah dey go for mah room,' said Tamuno. 'If you no come, ah will go look for man-power outside. You ol' man!'

Chief Ofubara sprang out of bed, seized a cane and ran after her. She led him into her room where she disarmed him and shut the door on him. He had no alternative but to spend the night in her room.

The following night, Jagua made sure she bolted

and locked the door. Tamuno knocked and knocked, and in anger went back to her own room. In the morning when Jagua came out into the sitting room, she could see and feel the hostility in the eyes of some of the other wives old and young.

One afternoon when Chief Ofubara and Jagua were preparing to board a royal canoe for a visit to David Namme in Bagana, Chief Ofubara instructed Tamuno to dress up Jagua in the traditional dress of Krinameh. Tamuno said, 'You never serious,' when it was her turn to cook Tamuno said, 'If ah cook again for dis house, call me mad woman.'

Jagua could see that Tamuno was working up for a fight. She thought, this little cocky girl. Me, to fight her? Many years ago, she could have fought any woman for a man, but now...Even when the children of the royal household, excepting the one who had welcomed her, were engineered by Tamuno to annoy Jagua into leaving, she kept cool.

The young man came into her room one afternoon looking very serious. Jagua asked him what was on his mind. At first he declined to speak.

'Tell me now!' Jagua pleaded.

At last he lowered his voice. 'I hear that Tamuno is planning to kill you.'

'Is dat so?'

Jagua told Chief Ofubara what she heard. The Chief summoned Tamuno and reprimanded her, but she vehemently denied planning anything so evil.

'Me — what ah go kill Jagua for? God forbid!'

Jagua was not taken in by her acting. She announced that as she did not feel safe in Krinameh she would leave.

The Chief said to Jagua, 'You must stay ... listen Jagua ... Tamuno, leave dis room now! ...

'Jagua! Is only with you dat ah kin feel am a man. Before you return, I don fit to cross any woman. You understand me?' He held her close. But whenever you stay wit me, you give me life, like say am a young man again. I kin never tire wit you.'

Jagua said. 'But your junior wife Tamuno wan' kill me for noting sake. And she done tell all de odders to gadder togedder wit her to kill me.'

'Don' min' dat proud gal. She no fit do anyting.'

'But,' said Jagua, 'Ah don' want you to drive away your junior wife because of me. Better for me to return for mah village. When you ready for me, you kin send for me anytime and I will come. After all, ah be your woman.'

'You be mah woman, true true. Don' leave me yet. Di trouble will pass. Dey soon tire. Don' go.'

'Ah tink say ah will come here and live wit you,' Jagua said, 'But now ...'

Jagua Nana debated within herself: to remain and be killed, possibly with some slow poison or witchcraft. Or to pull out, return to township life and trek the hard old streets again. Having seen Rosa and her husband, Jagua decided it was time to retire from the streets. She would rather starve to death than suffer that humiliation again. That chapter in her life was closed forever, so why not try to live with the Chief's wives?

She began by keeping to her room for two nights, but Chief Ofubara made demands on her during the day, and this was scandalous and unusual in the royal palace. The gossiping Tamuno spread the news and the Elders met and condemned Chief Ofubara who stared at them with bloodshot eyes and a bottle of gin in his hand.

'You do like say you never see woman,' the Elders reprimanded.

'Min' your business, Chief Kalio.'

'Because of your hunger for woman, small pickin' no fit enter bedroom for daytime you dey inside dey sleep with Jagua woman. You no fit wait till night come.' They laughed at him. They warned him to respect tradition and set good example.

Chief Ofubara threw a party for all his wives.

They assembled and ate rice and crab and periwinkle. Jagua was formally introduced to them. After the party, Jagua was accepted by the middle-aged wives, many of whom she found attractive and charming. Among the young wives Tamuno remained inflexible and hostile. 'Ah no like dat Jagua woman who come tief my husband,' She said to her hearing.

One afternoon as Jagua opened the door of her bedroom she felt a strange presence. The room was fairly dark but as her eyes grew accustomed to the light she saw a blackish object on the sheets.

Looking closely she found it was a calabash with feathers. But as she sat on the bed, a black snake suddenly uncoiled from underneath the calabash, a black cobra, the kind that eats eggs in the compound and bites a deadly bite from which few ever recover.

Jagua screamed and sprang for the door. When she woke up, she was lying in a bed in one of the rooms in a high fever.

For many days she was unable to find her voice but

when she eventually told her story, Tamuno was the
first to discredit it.

'Come hear o— ... Dis woman who wan' to steal
our husband, what ting again — o' Tamuno twisted
and untwisted the cloth around her waist. 'She say
she see one calabash, den snake jump from de
calabash and e no bite am. Where de snake dey now?
He fly or waitin?'

She gathered her friends together outside the room
where Jagua lay in pain.

Jagua was tired of the life-and-death strife with
Tamuno. She tried to get up, but was too weak. She
fell back against the pillows. Chief Ofubara walked
into the room.

'Tamuno — what is de matter ... what you dey do
outside there?'

'My lord, noting.' Tamuno could be very sweet
when she wanted to be her charming best.

'Noting ... You don't know say Jagua woman no
well?'

'No my lord,' still smiling and making eyes.

'Tamuno, come here.'

She walked towards him, breasts bouncing, head
cocked to one side, a smile on her face.

'Stand there!' She stood with one hand on her hips.
From the half open door, the other wives peered.

Tamuno had always been despised by them for
parading herself as a sex symbol. Secretly some of
them were happy that a stranger was challenging her
in her own field.

Chief Ofubara had discovered her among some
dancers after the first departure of Jagua and had
indicated that he favoured her. Arrangements were

30

made with her family and she became one of the Chief's wives. In bed, she satisfied him; but the gossip was that she was barren. Jagua had heard this rumour from one of the wives.

In two years she had produced no child. There was a strong rumour that she spread her favours to the young men in Krinameh. The name of one civil servant who came to Krinameh from the local government Council Office of Opobo was closely linked with hers. Added to all this was her arrogance and lack of manners.

Chief Ofubara said, 'Ah notice dat since de Jagua woman come here, everyday fight, fight. Why? Or you tink say I no see?'

'Me, fight, my lord? She's de one looking for trouble.'

'Is fight, fight, fight ... Listen to me Tamuno. Ah like you, das why I marry you. But as ah marry you, so I get power for marry anodder woman dat I like. Ah tell you dat ah already complete everyting' wit dis Jagua woman. Whedder she stay for Krinameh or she go back for her town, na my wife she be. If you worry dat Jagua woman again, you sef mus' to return for your Papa ... You kin den be free to follow all dos young bastard wey dey write you love letters.'

'Ah don worry her my Lord.'

'Good! ... Ah glad for dat.'

He watched her walk away with her usual rolling of the hips. Until the return of Jagua, these sensual movements had no effect on him, but now he began to feel the heat creeping back into his loins. He shook his head.

Tamuno went to her friends and swore that Jagua

must leave or she would never rest. She said, 'What de ol' Chief want from dat ol' woman? She no fine pass me! Even self, I fine pass am. Ah be young woman. Mah womb open for bring new pickin'. Her womb don close.'

One of the wives said to Tamuno, 'Make you talk softly. You dey fine palava. You know say Chief Ofubara love dat woman too much. Even self, he use to call am *Queen*. De woman get experience of de worl' pass you, Tamuno.'

Tamuno's eye blazed on hearing those words. 'Ah want make she die!' she hissed.

'No talk like dat. Person no be God. Na God give life, na God take am back. Not person.'

Tamuno stamped her feet on the floor. She began to sing in a loud high voice, disturbing everyone. She went before her mirror, splashed make-up on her face, put on her English high heeled shoes, which she had not done for some time, and left the palace.

The other wives whispered. 'She dey go see her lover. Ah hear say de man come from Opobo and he lodge for hotel.'

Another said, 'Dat gal — ah don't know what she want from life. She just dey wakka from one man to de odder. Das why she no fit born pickin. She dey mix blood too much.'

A small boy who was kicking a ball followed the ball into the room where women were speaking.

'Mama! Auntie dey fin' my palava.'

'Which Auntie?'

'Tamuno.'

'Hey, sometime dat gal head no correct. What thin' dey worry am? She fight Chief, she fight wit'

Jagua woman na him one go stay for dis worl'?
Sometime she craze. Gari don pass water!'

Tamuno, head held high, stepped gingerly along a
narrow lane, glancing over her shoulders to ensure
she was not being followed, and minutes later,
ducked under a thatched roof.

She stood for some moments not sure whether the
man she sought was at home. When her eyes grew
accustomed to the light, she saw the medicine-man
seated in the corner. 'Ah, Tamuno... you come here
for day-time? What happened?'

She sighed and sat on a worn stool hewn out of
timber.

'Someting happen... De medicine you gave me
never work!, and he cost me plenty money. Ah no
owe you anytin' now.'

'Tell me,' croaked the medicine man from his
smoky corner.

'De woman sick, das all, she no die.'

The medicine man laughed a frog laugh. 'You self!
Ah tink ah tell you when you come here. My hand no
dey for *kill* any person. Ah no be God. Ah no go kill
anybody. You hear me?' His face became set in a
stern expression. 'What tin' small gel like you wan'
kill somebody for? Abi becos de worl' don spoil? Why
you wan' kill somebody for? Make de person die,
make you one remain for dis worl', you go fine pass
everybody! You go get money pass everybody. You
go marry all de men for dis worl', you one! Not so..?'
He was mixing something in a bowl. 'Make ah tell
you sometin'. To kill somebody no good. If ah do dat,
God no go like me again. Dem no teach me for kill

any person. If you kill person, God no go sleep. **Look**, you young gel. Your mind black like coal tar. God don bless you, you fine. Any man way see you, must like you. But you want to wicked somebody. And I say, dis not good. My hand no dey for inside.'

The words cracked the silence. Accusing fingers stabbed at the musty air of the ill-ventilated room. Tamuno stared back like someone in a spell, mesmerized into tears by the medicine man's glazed and lifeless stare.

'Ah beg-o!' she pleaded, flinging herself on the floor, rolling about and screaming. She felt the medicine man's touch on her cheeks. As he leaned over her, she cleverly tripped him and brought him down. He fell on her and she entwined herself around him, still screaming.

'What you wan' do?' cried the medicine man in panic. 'Come and see-o!'

Tamuno twisted and wrestled with him and the door opened but darkened immediately with the face of the medicine man's wife. Her searching eyes looked from Tamuno to her husband and then turned away.

Tamuno rose before the medicine man and slipped away through the back lanes to return to the royal palace. In the sitting room she found Jagua and Chief Ofubara seated, talking. She noticed the two suitcases lying beside Jagua and the serious look on Jagua's face. Jagua was waving her arms animatedly as she talked and Chief Ofubara appeared to be pleading with her.

Then Tamuno overhead the Chief saying, 'You will come back?'

At that moment, Tamuno froze where she was standing by the door to her own room.

'Is better for me to wait till you come look for me when you want me,' Jagua said. 'Ah will give you de address of my Brother Fonso for Onitsha market.'

She opened her handbag, and after a quick search, produced a slip of paper which she handed over to Chief Ofubara. He tried to read it, then called a boy to fetch his reading glasses.

Tamuno was about to slip away, satisfied, when Chief Ofubara called out to her. 'Tamuno, come here.'

Tamuno tip-toed and stood before them, her eyes dancing with mischief.

'Tamuno, how many years you be before ah marry you?'

'Ah reach twenty years.'

'So you be young gel, not so?'

'Na so, my Lord.'

'You be virgin when ah marry you?'

She let that pass.

'You no hear me?'

She was silent. Chief Ofubara rose threateningly, but Jagua held him back. 'No beat am, na small pickin' dey worry her.'

'Small pickin', wetin? So dis gel never know dat ah fit to marry any woman ah like? Why she dey make juju for you? Lissen to me, Tamuno! Ah want to tell you sometin. Today you go return to your papa. Today, today! ... You see dis woman here? You know her?'

Tamuno started fidgeting. 'Lissen. Dis woman you see here. Na dis be only woman who always make me

feel like young man. When ah sleep wit' am, ah no
dey tire. She give me what man want. And she cook
well, better dan you wit your trouble and palava.
And...lissen, 'E no finish dere. When de woman
come here las time, me and my broder Chief David
Nname, de *Yaniba* of Bagana, we dey for big palava.
Even self we never talk to ourself for many years.
Krinameh people no dey go for Bagana. Bagana
people no dey come for dis Krinameh. No be Jagua
Nana settle de quarrel? Where you dey for dat time?
Abi dem never born you sef? So you tink that
because your bobby stand and you dey shake your
nyash, den everytin' you want you mus get am? Ah
tink say you dey crase! And ah must to punish you.'

His eyes blazed, his lips foamed, and he was almost
short of breath, but he continued. 'Jagua no come
here to tief your husband. Dis woman you see here
know about the world more dan you. When she bring
me and Yaniba togedder and our quarrel finish, and
our people make big feast, she glad and go home. Ah
send message myself make she come back because she
know how for look after me. You be small pickin'.
You tink say de thin' between man and woman only
for night, not so? Ah be ol' man. When ah like woman
is not only for sleep. Jagua be complete original
woman. As you dey see am so, no man pass am. She
travel de whole worl', Ghana, na dere dem begin call
her Jagua, England, America, everywhere! So,
Tamuno, ah want you to take your hand commot
from Jagua eye. You hear me?'

The other wives of Chief Ofubara of Krinameh
came into the sitting room. They heard the
commotion and guessed what was coming.

'Chief dey vex for Tamuno,' said one.
Another said 'He don sack am. Dat gel too proud.'
'Na lie!' said another.
'You go see who talk lie!'
Jagua said, 'Chief, you praise me too much, but ah tenk you. Not because of dis small gel ah wan' go back. Sometin' dey trouble my mind. Lef' Tamuno! She be small gel, who never see de worl'... Ah want to tell all of you here de reason ah want to leave. Ah hear some news about one my own pickin who I born when I be young gel like Tamuno. Dat time ah never know anytin' about the worl'. After ah born de pickin ah tink say de pickin die but now ah dey hear some story like say de pickin no die.'

A sigh escaped the listeners. 'Na God's work!... We praise God. Make the story be true...'

'When ah hear say de pickin die, ah tell God, "na you give me pickin, na you take am. Ah bless your name." Na him ah hear dis news again say de pickin no die. Ah dey hear like say some woman tief my pickin. She no fit get belly so she tief my pickin an' tell me say de pickin don die, she take my pickin give her husband say na him born am...'

Another sigh escaped all the women. Some of them cursed loudly. One of them openly reproached Tamuno.

'When woman no born pickin, however she fine, she be notin. Woman mus' to born pickin. She never do her work if she no born pickin. Das why, when ah hear say my first pickin no die, ah wan' to go and see whedder na true. Not because of Tamuno.'

Jagua stood up and looked Tamuno over with that disdain which only a woman can inject into a look against her rival. 'Tamuno, ah want you to stay wit chief here. De chief be good man. Born pickin for am. Take your hand commot from juju and bad medicine. What you wan' kill me for? De worl' is not for only one person. Keep your womb for Papa to put seed inside, not all those rascal boys in de street wey de smoke *wee wee* and drink OHMS like say he be water. If dem conceive you, you go born tief and rascal like 'dem. You wan tiefman blood for Chief Ofubara royal family? Is bad! If you no wan stay here, den go. If you wan' stay, have patience. Pickin' go come when God say make he come. Finish! Ah no get anytin' more for tell you.'

She turned away from Tamuno who was now weeping openly. All the women surrounded Jagua and hugged and embraced her. She patted the heads of the children and gave them money and spoke softly to them.

Tamuno stood desolate and abandoned.

Chief Ofubara put on his tall Victorian city hat in the manner of the Rivers chiefs and led Jagua to the waterside and saw her into the royal canoe. He gave her two stalwart men as paddlers and bodyguards with instructions to see her into a chartered taxi in Port Harcourt.

Amid much hand waving and beating of drums, the outboard engine sprang into life and the boat slid gently into the water and was soon speeding towards Port Harcourt and away from Krinameh.

Jagua waved back. She said to herself. 'Every disappointment is a blessing, one door close — anodder open.' This had always been the philosophy of Jagua and it was too late now to change. They sped past **Bagana** on the west side where David Namme, the Yanibe of Bagana and Father of her late great lover, Freddie Namme lived. It would have been good to call there, but there was little time to spare.

From Ogabu, Jagua travelled to Onitsha. She went straight to Brother Fonso's store in Old Market Road where she found him deep in negotiations with a number of customers.

'Welcome, sister.' He embraced her but his eyes were still on his customers. 'Sit down. I'm coming.' He offered her a seat.

'Brother Fonso, do you ever rest?' Jagua asked.

'Onitsha Traders do not know what is called rest.' He smiled. 'Just a moment' he said, and returned to his customers.

They stood by the warehouse which was packed to capacity with new *Honda* 175 machines. They appeared to agree on prices. He ordered the pick-up van to reverse into the warehouse and put on board one dozen motorcycles.

'This cheque you gave me...'

'It will not bounce,' said his customer. 'Is it today I've been trading with you or what?'

Fonso laughed uneasily.

The young men continued to load the motorcycles into the van. Fonso and a young lad helped them. Jagua sat watching.

'We are sure to come back for more next week,' said the bearded man who appeared to be the buyer.

'I shall wait for you,' said Fonso. 'Just be careful of armed robbers on the highway, that's all. If you hurry now, you will not have to risk travelling in the darkness.'

'Our worry is the delay on the Niger Bridge.'

'Well, can't be helped. It's the expansion programme. Things will be back to normal when the construction is completed.'

The bearded man came over and shook hands. He extended his hand to Jagua. 'Goodbye, Sister.'

Fonso said, 'Please do no be angry with me. This lady you see here is my senior sister... They call her Jagua Nana.'

'Oh!... The woman who shake the world. I thought so! I heard about her. Very famous!' He looked more closely at her jewelled neck, the sophisticated hairdo, the elegant high heels. 'Welcome, Madam. Your brother has killed us with high prices. No profit margin left for us. But he is an honest business man. We prefer dealing with him in the whole of Onitsha. Ask him. Do I buy from anyone else? Never!'

Fonso smiled.

They entered their van and began edging into the traffic. Fonso heard the bearded man say clearly, 'That Jagua woman, na wah!'

Fonso turned to his sister. 'Let us go home now,' he said.

Driving through Onitsha was like waging war against enemy infantry. The handcart pushers were a little more stubborn than the motorcyclists, and the lorries thought they owned the world. The impatient trailers grabbed more than their share of the streets and the car owners, left with nothing at all, sometimes in frustration drove solidly against the one-way street not minding the protests from pedestrians.

Fonso sighed with relief when they finally arrived at his house. He occupied one flat which sat above a number of warehouses.

'This is a trading town,' said Fonso. 'We live on top of stores and shops. That way, the landlord gets more rent.'

'You are too many in this town,' said Jagua.

'It is always so in a town where money is in motion.'

He parked the car and they ascended a narrow staircase at the back. Fonso's wife opened the door.

'Welcome,' she said to Jagua, and immediately set about laying the table.

She had prepared pounded yam and pepper soup with fish freshly caught from the River Niger. The children were back from school and everyone joined in the meal. After eating, Fonso left Jagua with his wife and returned to the warehouse. 'This is how it is, always,' she lamented in Igbo. 'I never see him. If he is not in the store, he is in Benin or Asaba, on business, or in Lagos. I am a widow with a living husband.'

Jagua smiled. 'That's business. The saying goes, you do not stand in one spot to watch the dancing masquerade.'

Fonso returned in the evening, had a bath and put on his slippers and tied a cover-cloth about his waist. He was relaxed and at peace with the world. He sat on the big divan in his sitting room and Jagua relaxed in a twin-seater opposite.

'Brother,' said Jagua, 'You know what brought me here? I went to Krinameh. I could try to be happy as the wife of Chief Ofubara. Although one of his junior wives Tamuno was fighting me with *juju*, I know the Chief could protect me. But I said, let me follow up this matter of my missing daughter, Eliza.'

Brother Fonso said, 'You did well...That story Sister Heide was telling...It puzzles me...You know, at the memorial service in Ogabu, people were too many. There was no time to talk privately. And Mama was there. She would want to know...'

'True.'

'Where is Sister Heide now?'

'I don't know. As I gathered, she moves about most of the time. Sometimes she's here, other times, she's there.'

'Anyway...'

'We can talk freely here. It is over twenty years since everything happened, but we still have to be cautious.'

'Yes, yes, Brother Fonso...Now tell me what you know.'

Brother Fonso cleared his throat and stretched his legs. He turned to his wife who was at work at the other end of the room, 'Stella...please let me have some private talk with Sister Jagua...'

'I beg you,' said Stella and left the room. They could hear her playing outside and laughing with the children.

Fonso said, 'It is like this...Sister Heide was passing through Onitsha. She came to my store in Old Market Road. I was there, doing my business when she came. At first, I did not recognise her as Sister Heide of Jos. You see, it is such a long time...Then she called me as Mama used to...Alfonso Chukwuemeka Obi. Who could know me by such a

name, but someone close to the family? I looked at
her, and she said, "Don't you remember me? Am
Sister Heide." Then I said Oh!...I remember
Auntie Kate. The one who was mistress of a white
miner. But forgive me, it is such a very long time. "Oh
yes" Sister Heide said. You were staying with Auntie
Kate, I remember now. I did not question her much,
but she began to ask about our family. "How is
Papa?" she said. And when I told her Papa passed
away, she wept. "What about Mama?" I told her
Mama is there at Ogabu. She wiped her tears and she
said she wished she could see Mama...But I said,
why not? I told her about the memorial service.
Listen, I said, if you want to see her, I am going there
tomorrow for Papa's memorial service. Sister Heide
said very good, can I come with you? And so we
arranged for her to come with me.'

Jagua listened with rapt attention. 'What did she
tell you about a child? Brother Fonso, you are now a
man of family, so I can confide in you. I got pregnant
when I was barely sixteen years...'

She saw the sharp look in Brother Fonso's eyes but
carried on. I did not know it was pregnancy, I
thought I was sick. It was Auntie Kate who helped me
to keep that secret. At that time I thought she was
showing me kindness. I was very grateful to her. You
know what Papa was like — very strict. He would
have killed me, if he happened to know about it.
Auntie Kate became my Mama at the time. I
confided in her every secret. Sister Heide became
nursemaid.'

Fonso raised his hand. 'I am coming to all that,' he
said. 'You see? I could feel that Sister Heide was

hiding something from me. I decided not to rush her. I waited. And at last, she brought up the matter. She said "Chukwuemeka, there is something I want to tell you..." And I asked what it is? And she said, "It's about the rioting at Jos... Do you know your sister had a daughter? She left the daughter with Auntie Kate but I was the nurse. During the rioting your sister's daughter vanished after some thugs broke into our house"... I said to Sister Heide are you talking about Jagua Nana? She said, "Yes... Did Jagua Nana not tell you she had a child that she left in the care of Auntie Kate?" I said nothing. She shook her head, and said, "A pity indeed"... Sister Heide did not talk for some time. She was trying to decide something. When she saw how I was staring at her she said, "I am telling you this now, because you said Papa is dead. The matter can no longer be hidden. There is a proverb that says blood smells. One day the truth will come out. I won't want to be blamed." She coughed and said, "Your sister Jagua Nana produced a child, a beautiful daughter whom she called Eliza, and she left the daughter with Auntie Kate and continued to go to school in Jos before the riot came and most of the Igbo people at Jos fled for their lives back to the East. When I asked Auntie Kate what happened to the child, Auntie Kate told me the child died. I laughed. I could read from her face. It was a lie."'

'Any story from Sister Heide will be true,' Jagua said.

'Yes, you are right. Sister Heide is not like Auntie Kate. She is God-fearing. But where do we find her again?'

Fonso said, 'You know that she lived at Jos with Auntie Kate for many years.'

'You think she will still be there?'

'I don't know...'

They sat talking far into the night until Jagua noticed that Brother Fonso had dozed off. She nudged him. He opened his eyes, fluttering the lids.

Jagua went on: 'At my age, I have to be part of a family, my own. I want to settle down with some man, or live with my daughter. Time is not waiting for me. You are the only brother I have. You have married and raised your own family. Can it be that God did not make me as someone to marry and settle down? There are people like that, you know? Anyway, let me start by searching for this my daughter Eliza. Let me just meet her and know her face.'

Brother Fonso smiled. Do you think if you find your daughter she will still be a small girl? She may not even know you.'

'Doesn't matter...I will still know she is my daughter. I am already feeling hopeful, but sad. Am confused.'

A small boy came into the room. He looked at brother and sister as they were wrapped in deep conversation.

'Junior, why are you not sleeping?'

'I'm not sleepy,' he said, and climbed onto his father's knee. Brother Fonso caressed him for sometime. He whispered something in his ear and the boy happily left the room.

'Go and sleep in my bed, I'm coming.'

He walked the walk of a drunken man and entered a room.

'Family life is very good,' said Jagua.

Fonso said, 'Now, what we have to do is this. Now that we suspect that your daughter Elizabeth is not dead, we just have to try and reunite with her. This is not a matter we can report to the police. We must search her out and find her.' He paused. 'For a start, you must be ready to go to Jos...'

'Will I find anybody there, after all these years?'

'If you go to our old house and ask, someone may remember something.'

'But all the tin miners are gone, and their labourers. The tin mines are closed.'

'Not all of them... A lot has happened. But you have to take a chance.'

Jagua thought it over. 'If you say so, Brother, I shall go and try. Yes, I shall go to Jos.'

They let the matter rest there and retired for the night. Jagua rolled over in bed, unable to sleep. If it was true her Liza was alive, what was she like now? She tried to raise a picture of Eliza as she would look now.

She had nothing to work upon. Endless pictures flitted past. The baby was not even one month old when Jagua fled. And now she had grown through her infant years into a kindergarten girl, perhaps University... her father Nick Papadopoulous could afford to give her a good education with Auntie Kate prodding him on, and now Eliza must be a woman, with a love life of her own, possibly a husband... and ...children? No, I do not know her and cannot imagine what she is now.

It was almost morning when the mantle of sleep crept over her. She heard as from a distance the insistent knocking on her door. She recognised the voice of Brother Fonso's wife, Stella.

'Auntie Jagua, get up and have your bath.'

'Oh ... is it morning already?'

Brother Fonso's wife laughed. 'Brother has already eaten and gone to his warehouse.'

'I am coming, my in-law.'

One by one, the children came to the door and said, 'Good morning, Auntie Jagua,' as they had been instructed to do.

'Good morning ... You slept well?' said Jagua. She cuddled those to be cuddled and bade goodbye to those who were setting out for school.

Fonso's wife gave Jagua a large towel, and pointed to the bathroom where a three-gallon plastic bath of hot water, a bar of scented soap and a vegetable sponge were waiting for her.

Chapter Three

The Quest

Brother Fonso took Jagua to the Ochanja bus station early next morning. The passengers bound for Jos, Kaduna and Kano had already arrived and taken their places. He bought her a ticket, saw to it that she was seated comfortably and gave her his final words of advice.

'You are not going there to fight, but to search. Remember that. Be careful.'

She saw him cross the bus station and head for the blue Nissan Patrol car. The bus departed soon after seven, hoping to cover the eight hundred kilometres via Enugu and Makurdi and arrive before dusk.

'We will be at Jos by five p.m.,' said one experienced traveller. Jagua knew when they by-passed Enugu and Nsukka. She fell asleep in the air-conditioned bus and did not know when the bus touched Nsukka, Otukpo and Makurdi.

'Akwanga! . . . Akwanga! . . . shouted the Conductor. She opened her eyes and saw that everyone was getting down to stretch and relax.

The bus driver in his blue uniform announced a lunch break. Jagua came down with the other passengers into the hot afternoon sunshine and they were all immediately beseiged by Agents of the eating houses.

'Follow me! Ah get fine pounded yam with *egusi* soup!'

'Grass-cutter meat! Dis way! . . .'

'Fried plantain with rice and fresh fish!'

One of the agents seized Jagua by the arm and she wrestled free. Other agents clamoured and begged and tugged at the passengers clothes. 'Watch your handbag, Madam,' warned one passenger smiling.

'This is where we always eat on the route.'

Jagua looked round. It was a complete town in itself. Spreading over many hectares with parking space for lorries and trailers, there were petrol stations, supermarkets, mechanics' sheds, motor spare parts dealers, artisans and craftsmen of all kinds. They said it was built by one adventurous Igbo man who had left his home in the East, cleared the bush and erected sheds. He started on a small scale, but very soon, others joined him and the settlement grew.

A tall serious-looking man in immaculate sky-blue safari with a heavy beard, fell into step with Jagua and led her into an inner room. He did not solicit her or pester her. She somehow believed he must be one of the passengers, he was so cool.

The table was laid, the room was well furnished, and a standing fan wafted the warm air and stirred the light green window curtains.

'Help yourself,' the man said, and Jagua obeyed.

Each plate she opened startled her. Bush meat, well smoked fresh fish in pepper soup. 'We get the fish from River Benue,' the man explained. Pounded yam served in china dishes, rice prepared as jolof, with chicken.

'Madam,' said the man, 'Jus' help yourself. Am sure ah know you before.' A boy came in and placed

50

several bottles of frosted beer on the table, with long clean glasses.

'We use Honda Generating plants to get electric power...'

Jagua was overwhelmed. The man's eyes made no secret of his desire. They were fixed unwaveringly on the cleavage of her bosom.

'You say you know me?' Jagua said in her most coquettish voice.

'I tink so.' He lit a cigarette and drew on it. Jagua liked the manly smell of the cigarette. He was sitting in the soft leather two-seater, too comfortable for a transit eating house in the bush. Jagua was still wondering why this place should be so luxurious.

'One of my wife run away,' he said.

The voice came from some distance, from Krinameh or Bagana, or Gunle in Lagos. Memories stirred. She looked up and saw the wolfish look in his ravishing eyes. Bells began to ring in Jagua's head. Suddenly she pictured how it had been with Chief Ofubara on that first night, and the tears rushed to her eyes.

'Na your fault,' Jagua heard herself saying, 'when woman run away from man, na de fault of de man, always.'

He smiled. 'Not this time.'

'How many wife you get?'

'Ah get many. De work here is too much for one person only.'

He was gazing so intently at her that she felt undressed and tried to pull down the flimsy blouse over her breasts but his look remained steady. 'You never hear de story, and you say na mah fault.'

'Ah know how you men use to treat women rough, specially for bush place like dis.'

The man laughed. He had large gleaming white teeth, and she liked how he threw back his head and crinkled his eyes.

Jagua crossed her legs, giving him a quick flash of her thigh. He shuddered. 'God!' said the man. 'How a strong thick Madam like you can travel alone by luxury bus? You come from Onitsha?'

'You wan' make ah fly by aeroplane?'

'We no dey see people like you for dis road,' said the man. 'Special people.'

'How you know say ah special?'

The man said, 'Never min' how ah treat mah wife.'

'Ah be woman. Ah mus' min'. She no born pickin for you?'

The man said, 'Not pickin' ah dey fin'. All my pickin dey for college now. Das why ah come here open dis hotel...Ah need plenty woman who go work for me, woman who some man kin' see an' he know say dis place, na person get am.'

Jagua gave him a sideways look.

Encouraged, he sat near her and held her hand. The noise from the other eating places came to her as from a distance. She said, 'Person go enter-o!' and he said, 'No worry. Na me get this my special place. I tell you, you be special V I P!'

A thrill began to stir in Jagua's head and race down through her body. Her heart was beating faster in a manner she thought would never happen again.

'Oh my God,' she said under her breath, feeling some deep pain. She began to feel a cloud over her

52

eyes and before she knew it, two beads of tears appeared on her face.

'Why you dey cry?' said the man.

'Oh God, ah don' know why ah dey cry.'

He put his arm over her shoulder tenderly and a handkerchief appeared in his hand. 'Clean your face, Madam.'

She sniffed the manly perfume and cleaned her face and leaned on his chest. She felt completely at home on that chest. How had it all happened so fast? Was this magic?

'Come make you go see de place ah live.'

'Motor go leave me-O!' She said in a small voice.

'Never min'. Motor go, motor come. You go get anodder luxury bus. Dem pass here all de time. Day and night, non-stop.'

He took her to the other side of the eating place. The driver of the luxury bus was horning and tooting for Jagua to come along, but Jagua waved at them. She was carrying only a small hand-luggage and did not need to go back to the bus.

'Make una dey go! Bye-bye!'

The passengers climbed aboard. Jagua waved. She watched the luxury bus drive off, blue and gold with the legend OPPORTUNITY KNOCK ONE TIME blazoned across the front. She waited for the dream to pass. It was no dream. She was standing in the Akwanga eating place and this strange handsome man was taking her round. It was magic. The bus had turned a corner and other buses, new arrivals, were coming in and parking. The passengers were being besieged by caterers and their agents. Life was rolling and recycling.

They walked across a cleared area. A boy ran
towards them. 'Welcome, Masta,' said the boy. A
voice warned Jagua that what she was doing was
stupid and crazy. A man she had never met in her
life, a man whose name she did not know, a man who
had no address, but lived at the crossroads of the
Nigerian Highway system, was taking her into his
bedroom and she had abandoned her journey and
was following him like a sheep, without question.

He now lowered his voice, so she had to strain to
hear him.

'Ah want you to rest for small time. If you like dis
place, then you can stay wit me. You will help me for
dis work.'

He took her to the back of the yard where, to her
amazement she saw an extensive poultry farm.

'Is not hard to raise chicken. We get five thousand
egg every day. We use to buy our feed from Lafia or
Jos, but is better to have your own feed mill. From
here to Jos is only about two hour for motor, even less.
Ah get one driver and one pick-up van and one
mercedes lorry. As ah see you, my spirit jus' like you.'

'Myself, ah like you,' said Jagua.

She looked at him again more closely. He was a
man in his late forties, muscular, moustached and
well groomed. He spoke with confidence. This was a
man who had seen life and had made his choice. She
still did not know his name or where he came from,
but he appeared to be a man from the Eastern part of
Nigeria.

She was still too shaken by surprise. She heard him
say, 'If you say no, den ah know say God no like me.'

To stay here would mean — No! She could

not . . . what would she tell Brother Fonso? But — slim chance though it was — this place was situated at the crossroads of the country. She might one day find Auntie Kate eating in one of the eating houses. It was possible. Or she could easily take some time off to visit Jos, using Akwanga as her base.

'Ah go tink about dis matter,' she said.

For the first time since the death of Uncle Taiwo, Jagua slept soundly. She woke in the arms of the stranger, expecting the spell to be broken, but it was still there. She was wearing a transparent blue nightgown trimmed with lace. He lay beside her, tracing the outline of her breast.

'Ah never know your name,' he said.

'Meself, ah never know your own.'

Jagua thought, 'We are behaving like small pickin'. She said, 'My name be Jagwah.' And she gave him a piercing look.

He sprang out of bed and leapt like a monkey. 'What! Ah hear about one woman dem call Jagwa Nana.'

She was thrilled. 'Das me.'

'God!' He began thrashing about like someone possessed. 'You — Jagua Nana!'

She laughed.

'God! . . . De people way pass trough dis Akwanga! President and Governor and King and Queen! Dem will hear about you and come take you from me. Ah want you to stay. You hear me? Promise me!' He suddenly looked pathetic as though he would lose everything if she left him. 'Promise me, I say!'

'Ah promise,' said Jagua.

'Wait . . . Ah want you to promise again.'

'True to God, ah promise.'

'Listen, me an' you go be proper business partner. We mus' make some money.'

'Yes, we mus' make some money...' She thought of investing the balance of Uncle Taiwo's money which she carried in her travelling bag.

As if anticipating her, he said, 'Ah jus' want you to be mah Manager. De time you will put money in de business never reach. If you be mah Manager, ah kin get more time to run de business...'

She was silent for a moment, and then she said, 'But you never tell me your name.'

'Ah! I forget. He be like say me and you done know ourself since long time...' His face wore a serious look. 'My name be Tobias, Tobias Momah. Das my name, and na me be first man wey start hotel here in Akwanga, before everybody come rush in and spoil everyting.'

'Never mind! God's time na him be de best.' Jagua said.

In the morning, Tobias came into her room.

'You sleep well?' he asked.

'Oh yes, but mosquitoes.'

He smiled. 'Dem plenty... We get mosquito coil, and we get shelltox. If you burn mosquito coil, you cough. If you spray shelltox, mosquito will die until breeze blow de spray commot from your room and anodder mosquito go come when you sleep. If you close window, you choke yourself.' He shook his head. 'What will man pickin' do?'

'Mosquito na problem,' Jagua smiled.

'But mosquito be our friend. Na mosquito drive white man from West Africa. Das why dem give we independence. Not like South Africa where dem refuse to lef' black man country because no mosquito.'

They both laughed. He sat down by the bed.

'Jagua,' he said, taking her hand. 'Tell me someting.'

'Yes?'

'Why you don' stay permanent wit any man?'

She smiled. 'I don' stay permanent wit any man...because de man Freddie Namme who ah wan' to stay permanent wit done die.'

'So you won't say permanent wit me?'

'Ah don't know. Is hard for Jagua woman to stay one place. Someting dey move inside my body, make me want to move always.'

He said, 'So you no go fit stay here? Jagua woman no fit stay for bush town?'

'Make we try first... You see, when Jagua woman stay wit man, first time, everting' sweet. Den small by small de sweet go begin sour, till 'e bitter. When dat time reach, Jagua woman mus' find anodder man.' Tobias Momah sighed. 'When you wake, I go take you round to greet odder people who work here.'

'Make 'e be for evenin' time. Make we work first.'

Jagua swung her feet off the bed and stood before the full length mirror against the wall. Her one-God-given body never aged, that hour-glass body of hers with the narrow waist and shapely hips, seemed to improve with the years. Her breasts had become permanently moulded, never drooping, full, but still not standing like a teenagers. Her skin glowed with youthful lustre. Her face had no lines and her eyes were large and appealing. She had a mane of hair which gave her that queenly dignity which awed some men, but drew respect from many. She was Jagua and ever would be.

By the time she joined Tobias, lorries were driving into the compound and passengers were pouring out to eat and drink. They ran straight to 'Tobias Hotel' and made themselves comfortable. At every hour of the day or night, what these toughened road travellers demanded was *gari* with *okro* soup, or *ogbono* soup, or if that was finished, *egusi* soup. They ate their *gari* in large chunks like famished men, wiping their plates clean, and drank beer straight from the bottle. Few drank minerals.

Generating plants were running all day and night. Tobias had a 12.5 KVA Lister fuelled with diesel oil. He said it was cheaper and less troublesome than petrol-engined generators, but most of the others used the Honda generators and never complained. Tobias had wired his own compound and those of some of his neighbours, for which they made a contribution to the purchase of diesel and the normal routine maintenance of the plant. Fridges and fans were in plentiful supply and at night the settlement gave a glow to the savannah from a distance, and travellers' spirits were buoyed up at night when they sighted the thriving community with its warm promise of water, hot food, light and bed.

'Ah can see you're happy here,' Jagua said to him.

'Yes. When man build sometin' by himself, he mus' feel happy.'

'You ever tink about home?'

'Many time — I used to go home two, three times in one year. Oh yes!'

A voice interrupted them from the eating room. 'I am greeting you-O!'

Tobias seemed to know the traveller, for he came out, shook hands and bandied jokes with him. Jagua served the food. The traveller's eyes never ceased to lust after her.

'Ha!' he said. 'But Tobias, you are always a good businessman. Who be dis madam?'

'My partner,' said Tobias. 'She has been wit us over one week.'

'You are great,' said the stranger.

He ate in silence. More men poured into the eating room, and places were found for them. They ate and paid in cash and moved on and more travellers came. Each time Jagua entered the room, the men stared at her with undisguised desire. One man winked at her, but unfortunately for him, Tobias caught the wink and eyed him for a moment, but said nothing.

When they had left, he took Jagua into the room. He said to her, 'I see how all de men wan' to chop you wit dem eye.'

'Dem dey waste their time,' said Jagua. 'Am for you only.'

He said, 'Make you try. If we build dis place together, you will get respect, you will be de big Madam.'

She smiled. 'Ah 'gree...'

'Ah jus' fear dat when we finish dis work, sometin' will happen...'

'Like what?'

He said after a while, 'Is a long time now dat government begin to worry us here... If dem say dem want take over de place what we can do?'

'Take over — but why?' Jagua was startled by the thought. 'All de time dis place be bush, what de government do?'

'Dem never ask you dat one.'

'If dem take over de place, dem mus' pay compensation.'

Tobias laughed. 'Today or tomorrow?'

'But dem mus' pay compensation.' Jagua's spirits were sinking fast. It had been like this with Uncle Taiwo. Jagua had teamed up with him, won the election, but lost him. And now, history might repeat itself. With 'Tobias Hotel', she knew she was on to a good thing, but now dark shadows were already looming. When would she ever find that peace?

'Dem can't take over de place — just like dat, for notin' sake. What bad tin' you do dem? You dey open up de country.'

'Don' worry yourself, Madam Jagua.' She felt a thrill when he called her that. This man really respected her. 'Till de time come, no need to worry. Make we try plenty before dat time come.'

Jagua came near him and sat close. 'I mus work hard wit you. I tink I like you too much. When ah sit down, ah begin ask myself, what medicine dis man take catch me like dis?'

He laughed. 'No medicine at all. When ah see you, ah know say God send you to me.'

The days rolled by, and Jagua was in danger of settling down permanently at Akwanga. She suddenly remembered Auntie Kate, and all that Brother Fonso had told her. She became depressed. Tobias must have noticed it.

'What's de matter, Madam Jagua?' he said.

'Ah believe ah tell you sometime dat I want to go to Jos . . . No, not to run away from you.' She saw the look of fear in his eyes. 'I just want to go find one certain woman who do me a very bad ting. No, not one woman. Two of dem. Kate Nene and Sister Heide. Two of dem. I wan' to see dem, private matter.'

'I can help you dere,' said Tobias. 'I get plenty frien' for Jos. If you go dere, you mus' not stay long dere before you return.'

'Thank you, my man!' The depression lifted, her eyes brightened.

'What time you wan' go?'

'Soon,' she said, 'Soon.'

Whenever passengers came in from Jos or were going to Jos, she asked them about Auntie Kate Nene who once lived in Jos on Sukua Street, where they ran the horse races in the evenings and her sister called Heide.

She told them that the two women were well known at the time. Kate was a free woman who was very friendly with the tin-mining white men, especially one Greek man called Nick Papadopoulous. Kate and Sister Heide lived together in two rooms and a parlour.

Some of the people whom Jagua spoke to vaguely remembered, but no one was quite sure where the two women could be at this time.

'Jos has changed,' said one old traveller. 'Not only Jos, many towns in Nigeria have changed. If you go to Jos, you will not know the place any more. The burying-ground has been built over. New layouts have developed. The place has changed...too much.'

'I shall be patient,' Jagua said. 'I shall just be patient.'

Tobias called her into the room and she excused herself.

Jagua stirred, opened her eyes. Tobias was smiling down at her.

'Get up, Madam! If you still going to reach Jos in time!'

Jagua yawned and rolled out of bed. She looked through the window at the square. Flickering flames shone from a hundred *batches* and the portable generating plants set up a steady roar. Lorries were rolling in and out of the large square as if being pursued by time.

'What o'clock is it?'

'Ten after five. Soon the sun will rise and begin to burn everyting. You better leave by six. Driver don' baff and wash de car. Is waiting for Madam!'

'Ah soon ready, my dear husban'.' She hugged him and pulled him down on the bed.

A knock at the door disturbed them. 'Who's dat?'

'Driver, sah. Is Madam ready now? I wan' carry de bag.'

Jagua and Tobias disengaged. Jagua said, 'Wait me. I'm coming soon.'

It was still foggy when they set out. The Driver obviously knew his way and was very cautious, yet made good speed. Tobias had said to her, 'When you get dere, just look roun'. Have patience, make enquiries. Don't tink you fit do everyting same day . . . If you finish about five in de evening, you kin still return before seven. Try to return today. I shall be expecting you.'

'I go try come back in time,' said Jagua Nana.

'I must warn you. Avoid night travel, Jagua. If is late, spen' de night in Plateau Hotel, return in de morning. Das all, don' take risk.'

The fog began to lift from the horizon, revealing rock formation that no mad sculpture could possibly conceive. Huge tonnages of rocks were balanced against the skyline on mere needle-points and had been like that for centuries, yet had not fallen, but looked as if the slightest tremor of wind would upset them.

As she looked at the savannah and rock landscape, memories of her youth came rushing back and with them the tears. How often had she and her friends gone Girl-Guiding in the rocks, when the indigenes of Jos came down to the market from the Jantar rocks with their cooked groundnuts and *acha* and after selling would adorn themselves in cowrie-shell costumes and blow their flutes and dance. The rocks had not moved or grown bigger since those days.

Within two hours they were entering the town of Jos and Jagua could hardly believe her eyes. From the outskirts of town, she saw factories, biscuit factories, paint factories, rock-blasting factories, industries of different kinds, from shoes to soft drinks.

'What is dat fine house, Driver?'

'The Governor's house.'

'Where is de burying-ground?'

'Other side of town. You wan' to go there?'

'No,' she said, quickly. She remembered how

Auntie Kate had taken her there and shown her the
supposed grave of Liza Nene Papadopoulous her
daughter, killed, so she said in the tribal rioting.

The people of the town were just beginning to roll
to work.

'So many cars,' said Jagua, 'so few bicycles. Not
like before . . .'

'Long time since you come here?'

'Long . . . since ah been small gel . . .'

They penetrated deeper into the town. To Jagua,
the streets of Jos now looked smaller, shorter, after so
many years. They used to be so long and large when
she walked them with her small child's feet.

She asked herself what she had so impulsively set
out to find after so many years absence. Sister Heide,
Auntie Kate? What was the sense in looking for
Auntie Kate? That infertile woman had no iota of
sentiment. They stopped near a Mallam who was
tolling his beads under a mango tree.

'Ah beg, am asking de way to Dutsen Bako Road.'

He raised his head with its fine growth of silver
beard and examined Jagua Nana critically. 'Go that
way . . . You see that mango tree over there, near the
Giddan Sollo . . . Where those two boys are riding
bicycle . . . When you get there, turn right . . .'

The driver complied. In this part of town the foot
passengers threw themselves in front of the Range
Rover challenging death or injury. There was no sign
of the house in which Jagua's father had once lived.
She remembered where it once stood. There had
been an open space and it was across this open space,
on the other side, that Sister Heide and Auntie Kate
had lived.

But now the minarets and domes of a mosque rose skyward and men were washing their feet and faces from plastic kettles of water which they poured liberally, mumbling *Allah-ham-di-dillahi!*

A Mallam in a white turban came close to Jagua Nana.

'You are looking for someone?'

Jagua said, 'Mallam, I want to find . . .' The Driver cut in speaking Hausa. 'Was there a house here before?' 'We are asking about some Cameroons people who used to live here . . .'

Another Mallam came out of the Mosque and looked closely at Jagua Nana and at the Driver. He called Jagua aside. His skin was light, but his nose did not have the fine point of the Fulani men, though he carried himself with some importance.

'I see you are from the South,' he said. 'I too, am from the South, though I embraced Islam . . . Oh yes. And I am preparing for the next Haj . . . It's the way of life.'

'Welcome,' said Jagua, 'Allah be praised.'

'You wanted to know about Cameroons people.'

'Yes, one particular woman . . .'

'Things have changed. Listen. This whole town has changed its population many times. People come and people go. First it was the tin mines . . . then it was the riot . . . the Cameroons people have gone. The Urhobo and the Itsekiri people have gone . . . Many of the Igbos have gone . . . You know that many tin mines closed down for lack of business. But . . . let me tell you something.'

'Yes?'

'If you go to the National School at the foot of the

rocks over there . . .'

Jagua got back into the Range Rover and they drove to the National School. In one of the classrooms, a teacher was poring over some papers. He looked up and said, 'The school has closed, if you are looking for anyone . . .'

And after he had listened to Jagua, he said, 'I'm sorry, I cannot help you. The people you speak about are no longer here. After that riot, a lot of people packed and left.'

They drove aimlessly round the town. In the afternoon Jagua told the driver to point the car towards Akwanga. She leaned back and the car wound its way through the town and soon they were out and in the open. They had travelled about fifty kilometres of winding road bordered by breath-taking rock-formations. Suddenly Jagua noticed ahead of them, across the highway, a car parked diagonally blocking their path.

A check point? But it had not been there before. 'Slow down, Driver!' She remembered Tobias warning. The driver stopped the car. 'Robbers!' cried Jagua. Instantly the driver wheeled the car round. Jagua saw four men enter that car and give them chase. She was shivering with fright.

The driver of the Range Rover accelerated and forced the car through twists and turns while the tyres screeched. Suddenly, they were side by side. Jagua saw the two men sitting in front of the opposing car. One was raising what looked like a small gun and pointing it at them. Jagua Nana's driver swung his car sideways, risking everything and bashed the pursuing car sideways before it had a chance to overtake them and block them off. There was a resounding crash and next moment, the pursuing car spun down the hill and crashed among the trees and the rocks. Jagua's driver said, *Chineke*! Now he was trembling. His own car had not been dented. He turned the car and they returned to Akwanga.

Jagua was relieved when she saw Tobias Momah pacing up and down in front of the *batcha*. 'What kept you so long?' And then he looked closely at Jagua. 'Any trouble?'

'Robbers!' said the driver.

'For de check-point.' Jagua explained.

'Thank God, nobody killed.' He led the way. 'Come inside.' And after Jagua had narrated the story, he called the servants and ordered them to kill a goat and prepare a special stew to celebrate. The pounding of yam continued well into the night. A large headpan stew of egusi and bitter-leaf was boiling on the fire. *Mateus Rose* wine emerged from the freezer.

Late at night, after things had quietened down, Tobias face darkened.

'Whas de matter?' Jagua asked. 'Why you serious?' She had shed her clothes and was lying in bed, relaxed.

'Jagua, I won't hide anything from you... Information reach me say de Government want to demolish dis our place where we get our daily bread. Dis time is not a joke. Dem serious.'

'Why, now?'

'Dem say de place be *illegal*. We build witout approve plan.'

'So na jus' now dem know? Dem jus' wan' to be

wicked, dat's all. You don' know anybody you kin
talk to for de government. Sometime dem want take
bribe?'

'You know what dis mean? He mean we close down
and fin' new place.'

'God forbid! After all you suffer.'

They lay side by side. Then Jagua placed her arm
over his chest. 'Whatever happen, I stay here wit' my
man.'

'I go nowhere, because my last penny dey for dis
place.'

Jagua was already snoring.

Chapter Four

The Daughter

Liza parked her car outside the Cameroons Embassy in Lagos. The girl at the Reception did not smile as she gave her a form to fill. With eyes on the form she dialled a number and spoke a few words in a low voice. Her eyes twinkled in a smile. She passed the form back to Liza and stood up.

'Follow me.'

Liza walked behind her and was treated to a wiggling movement of the behind which could have interested any male. 'The Ambassador is not in, but the *chargé d'affaires* will see you.'

The *chargé d'affaires* wore a pale green French suit trimmed at the pockets with white piping. He smiled with his eyes.

'What can I do for you?'

'I've come to make an inquiry,' said Liza, taking the seat offered her.

'Anything to do with us?'

'Likely. I was at the lecture last night... It was quite interesting.'

The *chargé d'affaires* bristled with pleasure. 'Yes, we felt that with things as they are between Nigeria and the Cameroons, the lecture would be timely. The more the public know about the reasons behind the border clashes and how they occur...'

'Quite,' said Liza, not wishing to be treated to another lecture. 'I was impressed with the attendance.' She paused and looked straight at his eyes. 'I am interested in the Cameroons Community that came to the lecture.'

'Yes?'

'There was an impressive looking woman among them. Anyone would notice her. She came with a white man. When the lecture ended, the Cameroons Community stopped in front of the Ambassador to exchange greetings...'

The *chargé d'affaires* looked at the ceiling, prodding his memory. 'Just one minute.'

He went into the next room and Liza could hear him talking to some Embassy staff. When he came back, he said, 'The man with her is a Construction Engineer, an Italian by the name Alberto Ricardo. The woman, according to information, does not live in Lagos. She is a frequent traveller across the border from the Cameroons. She comes and goes often.'

'Do you know where I may contact her?'

'According to information, she does not normally spend a long time in Lagos before returning to the Cameroons.'

'I see.'

Liza felt the initial surge of hope vanish rapidly as she was informed that Auntie Kate might not even be in town. 'In any case,' said the *Charges des Affaires*, you have a lead now. You can always leave a message for her here and we will try to deliver it.'

Liza made a mental note to seek out Alberto Ricardo. It would mean going round to a number of Italian Construction Companies or even the Italian Embassy. It would not be too difficult.

She drove to her house in Surulere. The girl, Titi,

told her that a lawyer friend had called and left a note. She read the note and it asked whether she had a copy of Supreme Court Judgements from 1922 to 1927. The signature was a scrawl and she felt the message was in a code she could not decipher. She wondered who it could be.

Titi had also handed her an orange envelope, the familiar telegram envelope of the Posts and Telegraphs Department. The telegram from Saka Jojo said AM COMING HOME FRIDAY TAKE IT EASY. Liza smiled. It was good to be in someone's thoughts. Friday was only two days away.

In the evening she drove to the 'Old Bailey' Chambers located in Isale-Eko, a very busy and populous part of the Island. She was attached to a Senior Advocate of Nigeria Mr. Olusanya, who had been in practice for more than twenty years. His Chambers comprised five lawyers who were in and out of Lagos most of the time, seeing to cases in different parts of the country. They called it 'Old Bailey' to remind them of student days in England.

Mr. Olusanya said as she came in, 'Just the person I would wish to see.'

'What's new?' She asked.

'There is a case in Calabar which I would like you to handle. Here are your tickets, and here is the file. You fly to Calabar by the morning plane.'

'Oh, no-O!'

'Why not?'

'Can't someone else go?'

'I'm afraid not. Everybody else is out. Obi is at the tribunal. Hamza is handling the case of the students' riot . . .'

'Well . . . Oh dear!' She could hardly tell him that
Saka was returning from Brussels on Friday and
leaving town would spoil things. He would be very
disappointed.

'Madam, I'm afraid that's the nature of this
business.'

She took the tickets and the file and went into a side
room which she used as an office. She was soon
steeped in deep study of the case. By the time she
closed for the evening, she saw the line of argument. It
was not a difficult case, although one never could tell
the temperament of the Judge in any particular part
of the country.

It was late at night when she finally flagged all the
necessary reference books and bundled them into a
briefcase ready for the morning flight to Calabar.

Suddenly it occurred to her that while in Calabar
she could make some inquiries about Auntie Kate. It
was only a stone's throw to the border with
Cameroon.

She could not wait for dawn to come.

Chapter Five

The Stepmother

Auntie Kate was usually dressed like a film star, in pale blue or bright red or jade green, and her outfit was always European. She seldom wore accra cloth or george or lace or any of the other traditional attires, though it would have suited her marvellously. Her ears, throat, wrists and fingers sparkled with fourteen karat gold jewellery or imitation diamonds.

The hardworking neighbours in the tin mining town of Jos gossiped about her and always peered at her from secret shutters, waiting to see something sensational that would happen next, and they were never disappointed.

If it was a weekend, around seven in the evening, those watching would beckon to their neighbours to come and see a Ford pick-up van pull up in front of the pan-roofed house she occupied. Auntie Kate would gingerly climb in beside the white driver, but not before the horn had been sounded a number of times and the dogs in the neighbourhood had barked loudly and everyone had been informed that the white man, Nick Papadopoulous, had come to pick his mistress for the night.

Pick-up vans served the miners, the missionaries, the Reverend Fathers, taking them into the dirt roads on the Plateau, so the neighbours came to the conclusion that the white man at the wheel must be either a tin miner or a Reverend Father, or a missionary gone astray.

People soon knew that Kate Nene was the mistress of the particular man, that he was said to be a tin miner who had his abode somewhere in the Pankshin hills near the mines and outside Jos township. They did not know that he was Greek or that he was called Nick Papadopolous and they did not care.

It gave them a thrill to peep at the tall and long necked Cameroons woman as she stood for a moment at the door of her two room apartment, waiting to be picked up.

Kate and another woman lived together. This woman was called Sister Heide. She too was beautiful in her own quiet way, but there was something more domesticated about her. For this reason men were always proposing marriage to her, but she never seemed to want to break her attachment to Auntie Kate. They had been known together for so long. Auntie Kate was not the marrying kind and Sister Heide did not seem to understand that Auntie Kate would always find fault with any man who came to engage her.

It was Sister Heide who kept house for the two, scrubbing, washing, going to market, while Kate smoked cigarettes and varnished her nails and painted and manicured herself and wore the highest of high-heeled shoes at home and stalked about like a stilt-masquerade.

She usually tried to wake before noon, but was always in and out of bed most of the day, only to eat and go back again to bed. At about four in the afternoon, she would sluggishly wake up for the day and ask for something to eat to sustain her for the rigors of the pre-dawn night club life ahead of her. Sister Heide served her loyally and often without question. She would go to the kitchen to warm the soup, make the gari or fry the plantains with fresh fish.

It was only after the arrival of Jagua Nana's daughter that they would quarrel over who should stay behind at home to look after the baby and who should go to the 'Club'. When Auntie Kate would finally win, Sister Heide would accept without further question.

At three or four in the morning there would be a banging at the door enough to wake the whole neighbourhood.

'Open! ... Sister Heide, open!' Auntie Kate had a melodious voice and it appeared to any listener that she was singing.

'Open, Sister Heide!'

'Don' make noise, you will wake de baby.'

Such was the life of these two women at the time when Jagua Nana was an innocent teenager who lived with her father David Obi and her mother Martha Obi, just across the road from Auntie Kate.

From their own window, they could also see Auntie Kate when she came out to air herself in the evening. She usually sat on an easy chair, with a bottle of beer on a small stool, drinking, and when the men joined her, men who worked at the Secretariat or in the mercantile houses, the number of beer bottles would increase, the conversation would be more boisterous and the evening hours would speed by with greater intensity.

'We'll meet at the Club,' a departing admirer would say, 'Are you coming?'

'Sure,' said Auntie Kate.

It was at the weekends that Jagua always heard the sound of the Ford pick-up, and before it turned and parked, Jagua was already at the window, gazing at the dreamland style of life which mystified her and filled her with longing to be with them.

Jagua Nana thought Nick a handsome man, with his Tyrone Power moustache and his swanky gait. He wore a broad-brimmed hat and body-clinging trousers. He seldom crossed beyond the verandah in the daytime, as it would be most unusual for a tin-mining whiteman to be so familiar with people who lived in the *Sabongari*. But if it was dusk, he would clap his hands and cross that verandah and even sit in the padded chairs.

To Jagua Nana, Auntie Kate was a senior neighbour and that was about all, until the day when she was passing by and the woman called her.

'Sissie, come here.' Jagua drew near. 'Why you never used to greet me?'

'Madam?'

'Every time you pass here, you do like say nobody live here?'

'Good afternoon Ma.'

Sister Heide said from the room, 'Auntie Kate, the time be happas one. How you will know say na afternoon when you never wake before twelve every day?'

'Ah beg you, Sister Heide, don worry my head.'

She turned to Jagua. 'I use to like how you be,' She said. 'You fine too much. Whenever I see you, I use to glad dat you fine...You just return from school?'

'Yes Ma.'

'Go put your books down for parlour, come buy me cigarette and kola nut.'

Jagua was afraid of being seen around this woman. Buying cigarettes in the eyes of her father was a sinful act, smoking them, especially when the smoker was a woman, amounted to hell fire. Auntie Kate's over-familiarity shocked Jagua. Her father did not smoke neither did her mother. 'I don't know how dem sell cigarette, Ma!...'

'Jus cross de street, you will see dat Hausa man under de mango tree, sellin' cigarette and koka nut. Buy me some matches too. Have dis money.'

Jagua Nana took the money. All the time she had a feeling that Auntie Kate was scrutinising her body as a lustful man would do. She glanced at her own body and felt uneasy at the intensity of Auntie Kate's searching eyes. Women did not usually look at women in this way, only men.

By the time Jagua returned with the cigarettes, Auntie Kate had retired to her room. Jagua stood at the door, unsure what to do, terrified at the prospect of seeing the forbidden. Sister Heide said, 'Go inside, go meet her. She still sleeping. She take day make night. When everybody sleep, den she go wake up!'

Jagua stepped into the room which smelt of incense and myrrh. In her father's house, they sat on wooden chairs, placed on a bare floor. In Auntie Kate's parlour, the carpet was thick under the feet. The sideboards were filled with crockery decorated in the

77

oriental manner. Jagua wondered whether anyone ever ate off them.

In her bedroom, there was a large portrait of Nick Papadopoulous on the wall. Jagua was unable to recognise the young man who stood beside Auntie Kate in one other picture. Auntie Kate was wearing a white dress and the man was tall and handsome in his white felt hat.

'Come near me!' came Auntie Kate's ringing voice.

On tiptoe, Jagua moved nearer only to be more astounded.

'Na here ah stay,' said Auntie Kate, and noticing the interest Jagua was taking in the pictures, she explained, 'Das Nick, de white man who used to come here.' But Jagua was admiring the brass posts of the fourposter bed, polished to a deep shine. Auntie Kate had piled three or four layers of mattresses into the bed. Near the foot of the bed was a small stool for climbing into the bed and then sinking deep down, some twelve inches or more.

As it was, she could hardly see the young woman nestled within the four poster. Auntie Kate stirred, and the aromatic perfume in the room filled Jagua Nana's nostrils. It could be incense or it could be coming from the various bottles of perfume on the dressing table. There was an assortment of lotions, creams, powders all dedicated to making Auntie Kate more beautiful and desirable.

Jagua began to get used to the semi-darkness and it was a while before she realised there was a man in the bed, snoring beside Auntie Kate. She shrank back in shock.

'Thank you, my dear,' Auntie Kate said casually. She gave Jagua one shilling and said, 'Salute your Mama.'

Jagua never forgot that first visit to Auntie Kate. When she passed by Auntie Kate's front door, going to school and returning, she always hurried past, so that she would not be called once more and sent on an errand. Something inside her warned her to beware of that seductively beautiful Auntie Kate. She never told her mother of the growing relationship. Somewhere in the preachings of her father, she heard about 'sin' and 'slothfulness'. 'Out of the sweat of thy brow, shalt thou eat thy daily bread! It was difficult to see Auntie Kate sweating, though she did eat her daily *eba*, rice and salad made from the fresh tomatoes coming from the *shaduf* farms by the river Jantar.

On another occasion when Auntie Kate called her, there were half a dozen pretty girls whom she introduced as just coming from the Cameroons 'to find husband', and in the next few weeks Auntie Kate had 'married' them off to construction men and miners in the plateau.

At least once every month, a fresh batch of girls arrived, stayed with Auntie Kate, served her and moved on to their new husbands.

As a growing child who had been brought up by strict parents, Jagua Nana could scarcely imagine what racket it was that Kate was running. Once when Auntie Kate gave Jagua a pair of high-heeled shoes as a present, Mama said, 'Who gave you those shoes?'

Jagua had gained in height by climbing into them,

but she walked off balance and it amused her. 'Does it not fit me Mama?

'It fits you, but ... It's not yet time.'

'When will it be time?' Jagua turned this way and that, modelling the shoes. She had become suddenly more sexy and sophisticated.

'You're still a schoolgirl, though you have the body of a woman. You have to be very careful of men at this stage in your life.'

'I hear Ma.'

'Listen,' said her mother, growing more confidential. 'We are strangers here in Jos. Our real home is in Ogabu, though you were born here and speak Hausa well. Your father brought us here and we only came to do white man's public work, that's all. When Papa retires, we shall all go home and stay there.'

'Yes Ma.' Jagua was listening with half an ear. Her mind was filled with wild imagination. How would it be to go to the African Club with Auntie Kate so that she might be seen in the new pair of shoes. 'Why do you tell me all this?'

'Because you are growing up now; you are opening your eyes to woman things. But you are in-experienced. Men will deceive you. That is what I am warning you about.' Jagua was thrilled and confused. What will happen to me? 'Is it that Auntie Kate is a witch or what?'

Mama shook her head. 'Not so. All you have to do is put your mind more in your schooling.'

'I hear Ma.'

But try as she could at school, Jagua simply could not absorb the teachings of the three r's. Reading was a bore, arithmetic was beyond her grasp, and she could never sit down and write anything. She was always restless. The blood cursed through her veins with a warmth that made her want to feel the touch of men. And when the boys ogled at her shapely boobs and dancing behind, she felt even hotter all over and gave them encouraging glances. The bigger boys were always pinching her and the teacher once called her into his office and began fondling her breasts, to her delight.

Jagua was playing a game of ludo with Auntie Kate and Sister Heide. It was her turn to make a move, when they heard the blast of a car horn and the revving of its engine. The Ford pick-up pulled up and Nick Papadopoulous parked and waited. When Auntie Kate did not go to him, he decided to come over.

It was a warm afternoon, though the sun had started slanting towards the west. At close range now, and with the sun on his bronzed skin, his white regular teeth which he flashed in a smile and his agile athletic walk, Jagua saw that the man was extremely attractive. She got up quickly and began to move away, when Nick stopped her. He said to Auntie Kate, 'Who is she?'

'My frien'. My little frien'.'

'Quite a girl.'

'She be school gel-O! The Mama will kill you if you touch her.'

At that moment, another white man came into the room. Auntie Kate looked at him in some surprise. 'You be two today?'

Nick said, 'My friend is a miner from Consolidated

Tin Mines of Nigeria (CTMN). His name is James.'

'Hello, Mr. James,' Auntie Kate said, extending her hand and curtseying.

James turned to Jagua and Jagua felt the rush of blood to her face. She averted her eyes. He said. 'Hello!, and tried to find her eyes.

Jagua mumbled something and was about to flee.

'What's happening,' said Auntie Kate. 'Today be your birthday? Why you two come dis afternoon for this hot sun?'

'We have our monthly weekend party. You and Sister Heide and your friend here,' he nodded at Jagua, 'will come with us. You are cordially invited. You will all return home before ten p.m. this night.'

They came in and sat in the armchairs and Auntie Kate ran outside to send for some beer. She did not believe them about returning home before ten. She knew the miners' parties. They worked hard and played hard. More likely the party would go on all night.

'Jagua, stay wit dem. Let me bring some drink.'

Jagua sat still as a statue and said not a word. To every question, she nodded, or pretended not to hear, and this aloofness seemed to excite the two men all the more.

Auntie Kate returned and served the beer in those clean and beautiful glasses that Jagua had admired so much.

'What you decide?' she asked Jagua. 'You will go with us?'

'I want to tell Mama first.' She remembered the warnings her mother had been drumming into her ears all the time. Auntie Kate said, 'No need for that.

You soon return. Nick promise us to be home before ten this evening.' It could not be true, because once there, they would be totally at the mercy of the miners and there was no public transport operating at that time.

Jagua said, 'Will I go in this dress?'

'Leave all dat to me,' said Auntie Kate.

Jagua Nana felt the trap closing in on her. To go to a miners' party without telling her mother. If anything happened, who would be blamed? But what would happen. What was it that would happen?

Suddenly she said. 'It's Okay.'

Let the worst happen. It would be an experience.

'Why do you want a son from me?' said Auntie Kate.

They had just made love and she and Nick lay with his head between her breasts. He leaned back, lit a cigarette and watched its smoke curl to the ceiling of the bungalow. The air was still and very cool, which was one reason why so many white people preferred to live and work on the plateau.

Nick said in his deep baritone voice, 'It would be nice.'

'But when I am pregnant I will be ugly. You won' like me.'

'Some women are more beautiful when they are pregnant.'

'I will lose my shape.'

'Only for a while.'

He put out the cigarette and turned to her.

She said, 'You are not telling me de truth. Many white men use to come here. Dey get mistress or concubine. Den dey born pickin for dem, and dey leave dem and go back to England.'

'I'm not from England. I'm not an English man. I'm a Greek.'

'You're de same, white man.'

'No. You're mistaken there. Greek people like Nigeria. They stay in Nigeria. They trade in Nigeria. They marry in Nigeria. They give their children names of Nigerian people. It's different. The English people come here either as administrators or as master traders. They feel superior. They live in the reservations... *Tudun Wada*. They play golf or badminton, they employ "native" boys. Then, after eighteen months "tour", they go home to England and return with "home delivery" cars. They must never remain behind and "mix" with the people. They want to, but it's against their code.'

'But you obey de same law.'

'Why am I here?' Nick asked. 'I'm a free spirit; and that's why I want to have a child from you. A Nigerian child.'

'I'm a Cameroons woman.'

'You lived in Nigeria all your life. Cameroons is part of Nigeria.'

'True.'

'Cameroons and Nigeria, they live together, marry together, and so on. Now, do you want to give me a son?'

Kate Nene smiled. 'Everythin' is in the hand of God. Don' worry too much.' She tried to hide the fact that Nick's constant worry drove her into frustration. On the other hand, there might be something else behind it all which she could not tell.

'Now, I'm glad,' Nick said. He put his arm round

84

her and kissed her tenderly. **Soon he** was asleep.

Once, twice, three times, she had been pregnant for Nick, but each time, the pregnancy had aborted. She yearned so much to have a child that each time she saw a poor careless woman suckling a baby, she felt like stealing the child and running away. It was a strange irony of life. Some wanted children and never had them. Many had children, but not the means to care for them. Yet these were often the children that made their mark in the world. If only she would present Nick with a child and give him satisfaction.

She thought of what would happen if she failed. Would Nick take on another mistress? They had been together now for five years and she was sure his patience was running thin. She knew she must do something about it. What that was, she could not yet imagine. She was still struggling with the problem, when she too fell asleep, and in her sleep she was dreaming that Nick's body was intermingling with hers in one last embrace before dawn.

'Madam!'

It was Nick's steward boy and he was in the bedroom.

'Your tea don cold.'

Kate Nene stirred, yawned and rolled over in bed. 'Tenk you.' She glanced out of the window. The sunshine was already bright and warm. In the distance the rocks blurred the landscape and in between were the muddy little lakes, the creation of miners prospecting for tin. Labourers with shovels and headpans were toiling and singing. A pick-up van drove up, a white miner in khakhi shirt and shorts and a helmet stepped down and spoke with someone who appeared to be the Foreman. He gave some instructions, went back into the pick-up and drove off.

The labourers had excavated the banks of the river and produced the artificial lakes. The tin ore was being separated from the river sand to the rhythm of chanting labourers.

Kate Nene asked the steward, 'Where is de odder women?'

'In their room, Madam.'

In sudden panic she thought of Jagua Nana and what would happen to her, if her parents ever knew where she had been. Ten o'clock in the night had become ten o'clock in the morning.

It was bath time for Auntie Kate.

She took plenty of time, for there was little else for her to do. Surrounded as she was by servants, she could play the 'Madam of the House' to them, only having to whisper to have her wishes fulfilled.

At eleven o'clock, Nick came in. He took her in his arms and kissed her, while the servants watched.

'Not here,' whispered Auntie Kate.

They went into the bedroom. 'Why not?'

'The servants will tell story about us.'

'But they know that you're my ...'

'Mistress? But they already know ...'

'Is true but ...'

The servant coughed at the bedroom door. 'Masta wan' breakfast?'

'Damn!' muttered Nick. 'I suppose so. Yes, what you got?'

'Coffee, sah. Dem get fresh supply from Kingsway

Store.' He was always first with the news about new supplies.

'Very good,' said Nick.

Auntie Kate said, 'You forgot to shut the door.'

There was a knock. Samson was back again.

'De Foreman want to see you.'

Nick came into the sitting room to find his Foreman. He wore a steel helmet and muddy boots. He had some papers in his hands.

'For signature, sah.'

'Can't they wait? I have a guest.'

'No sah. De men are going back to Potiskum dis morning. And, dey want to get deir money before de bank close.'

Nick signed the vouchers and Local Purchase Orders. They were for tools and materials for the Consolidated Tin Mining Company.

'Ah!' he sighed. 'At last.'

Auntie Kate had changed into a very thin and shiny housecoat and as she came into the room, a slight breeze stirred it against the outlines of her body. The air was filled with a rich and sensuous perfume.

Nick said, 'I have to go back to the office. See you later.'

He took a quick bite of his breakfast and was off in the pickup, this time driven by the official driver. Within the hour the van was back at Auntie Kate's request to take home Jagua Nana and Sister Heide. Kate said she would be coming home later. She did not return to Jos for three days.

Every night when they retired, Nick talked about the same thing. 'I'll tell you…and listen very carefully.' He held her hand in his.

'You see, I believe that Nigeria is going to be a great country in future. Nigerians will have a great inheritance. I have lived and worked here for many years. I want to share in that inheritance, you see. And the only way is through having a Nigerian son. I could naturalise as a Nigerian but the man born a true Nigerian does not need to do that.'

'I don't understand it all,' said Kate Nene. She shook her well-curled head and wondered what it was that kept driving this man to this one wish.

'Don't worry, just give me a son.'

The need to have that child had now grown out of all proportion. Auntie Kate sought the help of European-trained gynaecologists. She went to native medicine men. She was sure that somewhere among them was someone who could give her the help she needed to please Nick and capture his love forever.

Scarcely had Auntie Kate returned to Jos than Nick was again tooting his horn the same evening outside the compound. She ran to the front door and saw Nick get down. He was again in the company of some friends.

When they came into the room, they said, 'Fine! Are we all ready now?'

'For what?' asked Auntie Kate.

'For the party.'

'All the miners are coming down to my place after our polo competition at the Club. They will drink and be merry and by midnight...'

Auntie Kate opened her mouth to scream. 'Midnight! ...'

'Or before then, they'll find their way back to their homes, if they can!' They all laughed.

'We want the girl with us tonight.'

'Not possible,' Kate said. 'Last time de mother nearly killed me.'

Jagua saw the way the men were looking at her. 'Come on,' said Nick. 'Bring her along! She was the life of the party the last time.'

'You go and speak to de mother.' said Auntie Kate.

'But you and Sister Heide will be there?'

'Oh yes.'

'Find us more girls,' Nick said, and he and his friends trooped out.

When they drove away, Auntie Kate had a quiet word with Jagua. She promised that this would be the last time. All that she was trying to do was to please Nick because he might soon be going away on leave. She also promised to speak with Jagua's mother and to reassure her that Jagua would come to no harm.

Jagua's heart was racing with excitement. 'What time?'

'About eight, they will come back and pick us.'

'I will try to follow.' As she said the words, Jagua felt a sharp pang of conscience. Everything inside her told her she was falling into a trap too soon after her escape the last time. But the urge to be there among the hard-drinking hot-blooded men with their coarse jokes and unconcealed lust was irresistible. Auntie Kate's pleading eyes and manner haunted her and she wanted to please her.

Finally, all was set for the evening. Jagua stole out of home when her father was out at a teachers' meeting. The company of Auntie Kate, Sister Heide and the three white men speeding towards the mining camp filled her with awe. She held firmly to the sides of the van as it tossed and galloped over the dirt road to the camp.

By nine p.m. the guests began to arrive. They were mainly bachelors, and the girls who came were Nigerian and carefully selected. Among them all, Auntie Kate and Jagua stood out resplendent.

The steward in white uniform served drinks. A glass with a slim stem was pressed into Jagua's fingers.

'Whisky. Drink up — just a little...'

Jagua shook her head.

'Try it, it will put you in the mood.' She sipped a little and spat out the rest. A glow filled her veins and hammered in her head. She suddenly felt like screaming with laughter and jumping up and down with glee.

Auntie Kate gave her a cigarette. It had already been lighted and all she was asked to do was to inhale, nothing more.

'It won't do you anything...' she was told. And she inhaled and the entire room rocked with laughter. The music was screeching and screaming from an amplifier. Jagua obliged and screamed. She shook the dizziness out of her head. A man seized her by the waist and began jumping clumsily up and down in what was supposed to be a dance, but Jagua did not mind. She yielded and clung to him. She felt his too tight grip on her hips and the pressure of his thighs on her thighs.

Other men were taking women and dancing with them. Some could not wait. They took the women into rooms and bedded them without further ado.

90

She had scarcely sat down when Nick picked her and
pulled her up. She glanced at Auntie Kate. She
tapped Jagua on the bottom and winked at her. 'Go
on, dance with him!' and Jagua followed.

Nick manouvered her into another room where
there were other couples in various love postures. She
smelt the hot whisky breath as he whispered to her,
saw the glint of lust in his eyes, felt the pressure of his
roving hands. In sudden fear she felt her shirt come
up over her face, and too late she realised he was
slipping off her under garments. Fear mixed with
anticipation threw her into confusion.

'Auntie Kate will be annoyed.'

But Nick was not listening. Jagua's terror
multiplied and when she felt the piercing pain, she
shrieked aloud.

'A virgin, my God!' Nick muttered.

No one would believe that with that body of hers,
the body of a mature woman, the 'come-on' manner
in which she rolled her hips as she walked, the
tantalising glances which darted from her eyes, that
Jagua was still a novice.

What was happening to her was a nightmare. The
breath of Nick choked her own breathing. Her body
was being crushed with the great weight of Nick and
suddenly, he seemed to collapse on her and she herself
fell into a trance. Her joints felt as if they had been
dislocated. She could not lift a hand or raise a leg. A
heavy weight held her down. She rolled over on one
side, slept, rolled over on the other side. She was
drowning, sinking down to the nether depths of void
emptiness and her head was one big hollowness.

She felt no sense of panic or fear or guilt. She just

lay there, drained. Where **was Auntie Kate? Where**
was everybody? Then she slept again. She was not in
Jos town, that she knew. She was somewhere outside
Jos, and she was fleeing and being pursued by semi-
nude men down a narrow lane and at the end of that
lane there was a high wall and she would have to turn
round and face all those men alone because there was
nowhere else to go.

Jagua's terror was neutralised by Auntie Kate's
coolness.

'What will I tell my mother?' she asked.

'Don' worry,' drawled Auntie Kate. Jagua
thought she detected a new twinkle in her eyes. She
must have known what happened the night before,
although afterwards, she and Nick retired to the
master bedroom. Was she not jealous, Jagua
wondered, feeling that the explosion would come
soon? But it never came. Instead, there was this smirk
on the lips of Kate Nene as though some plot of hers
had worked to her satisfaction.

'Papa will kill me!' Jagua said.

But Auntie Kate assured her she would arrange a
cover-up.

'After all, am your neighbour. You can spend
holiday wit me.'

They got to Jos in the forenoon. Jagua's father was
away at the school, and her mother had gone to
market. Their joint absence gave her enough time to
bathe and eat and settle down.

Since it was already past noon, Jagua did not
bother to go to school. In fact, the teacher of her class,
a dashing young man who had made secret passes at
her, came to the house to see her father and to report

that Jagua's attendance at school was irregular, and to ask what could be done about it. Where did she always go? The teacher wanted Jagua's father to be aware, in case anything happened.

When David Obi returned, he eyed Jagua but said nothing. That in itself was ominous enough. He might be postponing the explosion. At night, when she was relaxed and safely in bed, she would be awakened by the slash of the *Koboko*, the leather whip fashioned from ox-hide. At that hour none of the neighbours would be able to come in and intervene. It had happened before.

Her mother also said nothing. Jagua felt she was being ostracised. Later in the evening, her mother called her into her room.

'My daughter, where have you been? We have been looking for you everywhere, especially your father. He is very angry with you.'

'I went to Auntie Kate's place and overslept.'

'So you chose not to return.'

'It was too late Ma. After all, she is a neighbour. It is quite safe, safer than exposing myself to robbers in the night.'

Mama paused a little. Jagua went on, picking up hastily. 'I — I came back, I knocked, nobody opened, so I went back...

Mama smiled at the clumsy lies. She said, 'Take a look at this.'

'What is it Ma?'

'You tell me.'

Jagua examined the article. 'An underwear,' she said.

'It is your own, is it not?'

So Mama knew. Jagua felt her heart tremble within her. How had Mama found it? 'It is mine Ma.'

'Are those not bloodstains on it?'

Jagua stared at her mother. Memories of the previous night's orgy began floating back to her. She preferred not to talk for fear of giving herself away.

'Who is the man?'

'Mama, I do not know what you mean?'

'I asked you, was any man in intimate contact with you?'

'I don't know Ma ... We went to a party, and ... and ...'

'I was once your own age, Jagua. Tell your mother the truth.'

Jagua began to cry. She put her head on her mother's breast and cried. For once she realised that her mother had been a raving beauty in her own time. She remembered how her mother told her that Papa had to snatch her away from a man who had already paid the bride price and within one week would come for her from the North where he was working. In her youth, Jagua's mother out-danced all the other girls, was taller and fairer than most of them.

'My daughter, listen to me ... You are growing into a woman, very fast. You are already a woman. In our own time, girls of your age would conceive and bring forth. I do not know whether to advise your father that we send you to our home in Ogabu, to get yourself a man from a good family. You have refused to learn English education. You cannot also miss our own education, which is deeper than book knowledge. Know this: it is better that a man, one of our

94

own kind, takes you to wife. That can hardly happen while you are here. The danger is this: you may bring into this family a bastard child, and that is bad. You refuse to learn book. You now begin to sleep outside home, next thing, you will run away with some man and go and live in the tin-mines. That will surely happen if you continue your friendship with those husbandless women who are free-living over here.'

She listened to the gentle voice of her mother and she had nothing to say in reply. Should she plead ignorance? Should she say it was a mistake? Wherever she thought she was going, Mama had been there before her. This could be one advantage of having living parents to guide you.

'When Papa comes I shall talk to him. I shall tell him my plan to send you to Ogabu for some time, or even to Onitsha, where Brother Fonso is still at school. You can live with him there. It will be better than staying on here...'

But Papa had a different view. 'To whom should Jagua be sent? To Alfonso? But he is at school and is living with an Uncle. We cannot burden others with our problems. She cannot go back to Ogabu because everyone has left the town in search of white man's work, such as we are doing here. The people of Ogabu come home on general call, once every two years, at Christmas time. They will be home this year, and that will be in about ten months' time, God willing. That would be the best time to take Jagua home and plan for her... Until then, there is little we can do.'

To Jagua whom he called into the sitting room,

later, he said, 'You **are** a big girl now, and **I shall not**
beat you. But know this; the way you comport
yourself now, will determine what you will become in
future. If you follow foolish ways, you will become a
foolish woman. Do you want to become a foolish
woman?'

'No, Papa.' Her eyes were downcast, her hands
were intertwined behind her back.

'We are trying hard to make you a person, not an
animal or a vagabond. Your mother loves you, and
wants you to become a person she can be proud of.
She is a good woman, and you should try to be the
daughter of a good woman. But if you choose to go the
devil's own way, that is your affair.'

'I hear, father.' Of all things, Jagua dreaded to be
reprimanded by her father. It usually put her in a
sulking mood for days and days.

As soon as she left Papa, she went into her room
and locked herself up and would speak to no one. She
would not eat the food Mama prepared for her. She
went to school next day but her mind always
wandered away from her lesson to the men and the
tempting whispers in her ears. Jagua was aware of a
new interest in the male sex. Now when she saw a
man she felt an immediate response. Was he
handsome, or tall, or well dressed, or bearded or
moustached? In her day dreams she imagined the
appealing ones as her lovers. Nick Papadopoulous for
instance — if he was not already Auntie Kate's lover.
To Jagua it mattered little when month after month
she found that she missed her period. She did not
notice when on some mornings, she felt faint. At first
she reported it to no one. One morning on her way to

96

school the feeling came to her again. She went to
Auntie Kate who sat her down and gave her some
brandy to sip. 'It is nothing,' Kate said, 'it will soon
pass.' She was right. It passed. Sometimes, and
unexpectedly she felt a strang movement in her belly.
She went to a patent medicine store and was advised
to buy a worm medicine because she had been told
that when one has worms, the worms sometimes
move about. But these worms would not go away and
the movement continued, if anything with greater
intensity.

It was then she confided to Auntie Kate what she
was experiencing. To her surprise, Auntie Kate was
very pleased and excited. 'You sure say the man who
meet you be Nick Papadopoulous?'

'Is that all you want to know?' Jagua asked — She
had begun to acquire a new radiance. Her breasts
were rapidly filling out and her hips were becoming
more curvaceous.

Auntie Kate could hardly contain her happiness
because somewhere in her innermost thoughts she
had begun to hatch a diabolical plan for the coming
child.

She prayed it would turn out to be a boy child.

A loud cry pierced the morning air. Sister Heide
lifted the baby from the cot and changed the napkins.
'Sssh! . . .' whispered Sister Heide.

'What's matter?' said Auntie Kate from deep
inside her heavily padded bed. The man beside her
groaned.

'De pickin done wet herself. Ah change de napkin.
She don' sleep now. No palaver.'

They called the little darling Elizabeth. Liza for short. Elizabeth Nene Papadopoulous. Jagua Nana had managed it, a teenage pregnancy, a carefully concealed birth, a secret girl child hidden with a neighbour Auntie Kate.

Each time Jagua went to bed, she dreaded the thought that her secret would one day leak out. She stole there often to breast feed the child. Her breast was heavy and painful and full of the most delicious milk. When Liza sucked those breasts Jagua shut her eyes in ecstasy and joy.

'If to say you born a boy —' Auntie Kate said.

'We take what God give us,' said Jagua Nana who appreciated the help from Kate Nene without knowing her motive.

A card came from Nick Papadopoulous in Greece to say he was enjoying his leave and would be back in the country in about three months. Under the terms of service of the CTMC he got six months leave for every 18 months in the tropics. He had not yet been told about the new born baby because it was all planned as a surprise for him.

Tiny Elizabeth Papadopoulous was still a secret person who cried all night, changed napkins many times a day and sucked Jagua's breast milk with more passion than a lover would. Her nurse was Sister Heide and the part suited her beautifully. She never complained. Auntie Kate played godmother, and the real mother Jagua Nana was only a visitor.

Even though Jos was a peaceful town, there were sometimes undercurrents of tribal strife and when they erupted, hundreds of people would lie dead and the violence and fear would continue for a long time.

It was during one such riot at Jos that Jagua Nana and her parents fled the town. It all happened very fast. Jagua ran back from school and her parents told her to get ready, as a lorry was waiting. There was little time to take all she wanted to. Before her eyes, a man was chased into a well and the lid shut over the well. He must have suffocated and drowned there. Groups of killers paraded the streets armed with cutlasses if they were Igbo, or with bows and arrows if they were Hausa.

The lorry carrying David and Martha Obi and Jagua Nana departed at night. Before it left, Jagua jumped down.

'I forgot something.'

'Come along! Motor will leave you!' chided her mother, but she ran straight to Auntie Kate's house only to find it scorched with fire and deserted. She ran back to the motor station and found that her parents were in distress over her action. The lorry left without her seeing either Auntie Kate or Sister Heide or Liza.

What would happen to Liza, Jagua wondered. She determined that as soon as peace returned she would come back to Jos and this time, announce her daughter to her parents. This secrecy was unbearable. The new-born was entitled to her protection, love and care. Let them kill her if they would.

The rioting at Jos had finally died down and many people were returning to town.

The young Jagua Nana made a number of journeys to Jos before she at last succeeded in locating Auntie Kate in an entirely different part of the town. Kate Nene had moved nearer the Naraguta area and had found herself a two-room apartment with a verandah. Sister Heide still lived with her but was away at the time of Jagua's visit.

Auntie Kate embraced Jagua. 'Ah so glad you come see for yourself.' Jagua felt a loneliness within her. She dared not mention her inner terror. Kate Nene quickly went to the kitchen and came out with pepper soup liberally sprinkled with chicken.

'Ah know wetin bring you back . . . Your pickin' Liza.'

Jagua's heart took a sudden plunge. 'God!' she prayed.

'Siddown make ah tell you . . .'

'What happen?' Jagua asked in panic. She fixed her gaze on the shifty eyes of Auntie Kate. 'Tell me, what happen to my pickin Liza Nene Papadopoulous that I born for myself.'

'She done die,' said Auntie Kate.' God have mercy on de soul of de poor gel . . . Ah try, try to let you know, but ah no know where to fin' you.'

She went into the room and showed Jagua Nana a document. 'Dis one be doctor give me to hold.'

'What paper be dis?'

Dem call de paper *Death Certificate* . . . Das' de paper doctor give somebody before he get power to bury some person wey die.'

'Oh God! . . .' Jagua Nana shouted and began to scream and to thrash about the floor. Neighbours came in and held her. They tried to calm her down. 'Is God's work,' they said, although Jagua could have sworn they knew nothing about what was going on.

After they had left, Auntie Kate offered to take Jagua Nana to the graveside to give her a chance to

100

say a short prayer and to know just where her daughter was buried.

Together they set out in a taxi for the graveyard at the foot of the rocky hills. The public burial ground was guarded by a bent old gatekeeper who refused to let them in until he was convinced of their mission.

As he opened the gate to let them in, Auntie Kate said, 'You know why he refused open de gate?'

'No,' said Jagua.

'Because people use to come here to dig up grave. Them remove people body for make *juju.*'

'Oh!' said Jagua.

Auntie Kate led the way between mounds of earth which looked rather like ridges on a farm. Near one of them which carried a white cross and plastic flowers, she paused. Jagua read the sign: ELIZABETH PAPADOPOULOUS AGED SIX MONTHS. *R.I.P.*

'Is here we bury her.'

Jagua nodded and knelt beside the grave while Auntie Kate stood by, head bowed. Jagua mumbled a quick prayer then rose slowly, made the sign of the cross and walked dejected beside Kate Nene.

So, this was how life treated her. All the passion; all the suffering, and now — nothing. She felt like melting into nothingness.

As they walked, Jagua could not help noticing several open graves with human bones and hair beside them.

'Is this the work of the jujumen?'

'No, that one be hyaena.'

'Tell me! hyaena! What hyaena?'

'You see the hills?' Auntie Kate pointed. 'For night, hyaena use to come down from dere. You

know dat Muslims never use to bury somebody deep,
like Christian. Dem believe say man come for dis
world naked, so — man must go back naked when he
die.'

'Praise be to Allah,' Jagua said.

'Meself, I sometime hear de hyaena for night, when
I go to visit Nick. If you lissen well, you kin hear dem
fight over bone . . . Make you no fear, we bury Liza
for inside strong coffin. No Hyaena fit broke de
coffin.'

'Thank God,' said Jagua.

While they waited for a taxi outside the graveyard,
Jagua said, 'What you go tell Nick Papadopoulous
now?'

'Notin'. He never know anytin, so we go tell am
noting.'

'Is true,' said Jagua Nana.

Recalling that night of confused passion at the
mining camp, Jagua Nana began to doubt whether it
would be wise indeed to tell Nick that he had
fathered the dead girl.

'No need to worry about dat now,' said Auntie
Kate. 'God done do his own side.'

'I want to forget all dis,' said Jagua. 'Is a good ting
dat my Papa and Mama never suspect anytin' about
dis. Ah don' want anytin' to worry dem, because dem
love me too much.'

She stayed with Auntie Kate that night, her
business at Jos concluded. Sister Heide returned later
in the night, and next morning she and Auntie Kate
accompanied Jagua Nana to the railway station on
her journey back to Enugu and from there to her
home in Ogabu.

The two women dressed in bright, eye-catching clothes, unlike Jagua who wore a dark Accra dress and kept wiping the tears from her eyes. Slowly the train began to pull out and then it gathered speed and the window at which Jagua sat turned the corner amid the puffing and the belching of the steam engine.

Auntie Kate and Sister Heide returned to town. There was a repressed smile on the face of Kate.

Sister Heide asked Auntie Kate in anger. 'Why you tell de poor gel lies? You laugh because Liza never die. You jus' hide de pickin' from de mother. Why? You be tief?'

Auntie Kate said, 'Shut up! What concern you for dis matter?'

'God know say my hand no dey for monkey soup,' said Sister Heide. 'When de trouble come, no call me-O!'

'No worry,' said Auntie Kate. 'Nobody go call you.'

Chapter Six

The Daughter — The Quest

'You wan' taxi?'

'Madam! Take my taxi...'

The airport touts crowded round Liza and the other passengers who had just disembarked from the Calabar domestic flight. Already there were three other passengers seated in the waiting taxi, none of them known to Liza, but the driver did not mind. 'Go in...na de same way we dey go? Not Surulere?'

'This is like being kidnapped,' Liza murmured but squeezed into the taxi, as it was now getting late.

The driver got in and started moving, humming a song as he drove, with the radio full blast.

As they climbed the over-head bridge leading out of the airport, the taxi suddenly swerved and began to head northwards.

'Where are we going?'

'Is all right, Madam, I wan' drop one passenger.'

'This is not the arrangement! Stop the taxi.'

'If you want "charter" taxi, why you no say so?'

'Just let me get down,' Liza said, recalling the reported bitter experiences of late evening passengers at the hands of armed robbers. The sun had just set, and the sky still showed an orange tint — the moment before the street lights came on.

'But Madam, we soon get there.'

'You should have informed me.'

'Sorry, Madam.' He pulled to one side.

Liza got down, furious. The taxi sped off, leaving her stranded on a strange road.

Nearly half an hour later with the darkness increasing and stray men prowling menacingly around, Liza flagged down another taxi and this time insisted on being the only passenger. She was glad to pay more.

She was relieved when, within half an hour and in spite of the heavy Lagos traffic, the taxi drew up opposite her residence.

Titi met her at the door and took her bag. Ngozi and Obi were still outside playing with other children. On seeing their mother, they abandoned their game and came running to embrace her. She paid off the taxi, while Titi told her, 'Madam, Oga come look for you in your absence.'

So Saka Jojo had returned from Brussels.

'He said he will come back later.'

She took off her clothes with a sigh of relief, ran a hot bath and relaxed. She was wrapped in a towel loosely draped over her breasts and wondering whether she should prepare to go to Chambers when the door-bell rang. She opened it herself. It was Saka, resplendent as ever in a white Safari, white kid-glove shoes, a gold chain, bangles and that handsome smile of the play-boy extra-ordinaire.

'Hi, Liz.' His eyes lit up with lust when he saw her, barefoot, her hair in a plastic cap, her body covered only by a towel. He gave her one quick peck on the cheek, squeezed her, and as usual barged past her peeping into each and every room to make sure she was alone.

'There's no one there,' Liza laughed. 'When will

you kill your jealousy?'

'Listen, Liza . . . When women stop playing games. You are my woman and I want to possess you. Is that clear?' He threw himself into a chair.

Titi served him chilled wine. 'When did you get back?'

'One second ago. Didn't your spies tell you?'

'Spies?' He smiled. 'Whose spies?'

'The ones you've planted around me. You can afford to pay them . . . when did *you* get back from Brussels?'

'This morning. And I bought you something'. As he spoke Titi came in dragging a suitcase. 'Put it on the bed,' Saka ordered 'Thank you.' From his pocket he drew out a five naira note and rewarded Titi.

'Don't corrupt my maid, Saka.'

Liza noticed the amused glint in his eye and began trembling with curiosity. She snapped open the suitcase which was marked SELFRIDGES DEPARTMENT STORE.

'You passed through London?'

'Of course. How can a man go to Europe without passing through London? It's the only place one can understand and be understood.'

The lid sprang back. Liza drew in her breath. 'What! . . .'

Jewellery glittered back at her — chain necklaces and bangles of English gold, packed in velvet lined cases. But it was the dresses that stunned her. She ran her finger tips through three exquisite silk dresses in purple, black and grey, one of them — the black one, with a jewellery-studded belt.

'You must have an Italian girl over there who

chooses things for you.'

'Now it's your turn to be jealous! The truth is this; I tell my secretary what I want. She knows I have three wives and a mistress and she shops accordingly.'

'And the other wives get as much as this, each of them?'

'I believe in fair play,' Saka said. 'Even so, the prospective bride always gets the lion's share.'

Liza took him in her arms and held him tight. 'You are a great lover-man, playboy, macho man,' she said, and he bridled with pride while his fingers ran down her flanks tickling her into laughter, down her hips, resting tightly on her bum which he squeezed till she cried out.

'The front door is open,' she whispered. 'The children can come in...'

'Leave it like that.'

'Then let me shut the bedroom door.'

She moved catlike towards the bedroom door, as he tugged at the towel which slipped down, revealing Jagua Nana's Daughter in all her seductive innocence.

'Lord bless me,' he cried and began to get out of his white safari... 'Five days in that wretched Brussels. All they care for is how much they can fleece off you. It's awful...'

'Take me with you next time.'

'Why not? But I want to take you now, first!'

He was speaking to one breast opposite his face and after that he spoke very little or if he did, the sounds he made could be interpreted only by four-year-old children in wartime starvation camps.

'Saka,' she said after he had been satiated. 'I am a little bit worried about your wives.'

'Hm?'

'Your wives, I said.'

'What about them?'

'They are after me. I hear they have came here to identify this place. Saka, I don't want to be assassinated.'

'My wives are my business.'

'If you say so. But I know they are after me.'

'I'll take care of them.'

He must have slept off after that. She rose on tip-toe and began to prepare him a salad. The idea of chambers for tonight was out. She decided she would be there early in the morning.

When he turned and groaned she said to him, 'I have your favourite salad and a bottle of *Mateus Rose*.'

'Okay,' he said, and slept again, but only for a moment. She pushed the little table near him and he swung his feet off the bed and began to shovel in large mouthfuls of lettuce and cucumber.

'How was Calabar?'

'On the border with Cameroon. Remember we attended a lecture on *Border Clashes*. Well, after my experience over there, that lecture does not seem like a mere academic exercise any more. There is fighting on the border. It's going on all the time.

Saka looked bored. 'That's a problem for the government — not for me. I'm a businessman and I have no business with Cameroon refugees or slave labour or anything...'

'Quite right. You are the playboy from Carter

Bridge not one of the bush men from the minority forests.'

'Why should I concern myself with border clashes? You dragged me to that lecture. Do you now want to make me an Ambassador to Cameroon?'

'At least you should know what is happening in your country, so that when the war starts...'

'War!' He looked startled.

'Yes, war. How do wars start? — just like that. One day, you will hear about it. You will say I told you...By the way, I want to resume the search for Auntie Kate. I'm going to the Embassy tomorrow.'

'Good!' said Saka. 'And I intend to follow up the results of my own investigation. And I'll let you know.'

She put on a light dress and accompanied him to the door. He was eating her up with his eyes.

'I will be back tomorrow night, after midnight.'

'Please, I'm tired and I want to rest.'

'I'll not disturb you.'

'Who will believe that?'

'You...'

'You're a sex maniac.'

'And you are the daughter of Jagua Nana. What should one expect from you?'

'Is that why you are always peeping into corners? Your wives will kill you one of these days.'

'I'll go to heaven.'

'Hell, more likely. That's where all the money men go.'

'You're impossible!'

He laughed and unlocked the door of the BMW.

Liza touched the gleaming body of the automobile.

'You're making me too conspicuous, Saka. Why

can't you come here in your sports Mazda? Any sensible lover man with three wives would be more discreet.

'Because I'm going to a secret meeting from here and it will not do to walk.'

'What's so secret about a BMW?'

He slipped into the car and the engine blasted into a full-throated roar. The inside of the BMW was upholstered in immaculate white. Saka swung the car and shot forward.

Liza noticed the windows in the surrounding houses shutting slowly. The neighbours had been spying on her.

As she left the Cameroons Embassy, the Receptionist who had wiggled her behind at Liza, cornered her.

The girl approached, and looked over her shoulder. 'The woman you are looking for...'

'Yes?'

'She used to come here from Cameroon, and she lodges in one place in Balogun Square ... wait! I'll give you the address.'

She stepped gingerly back to her desk, rummaged and came up with a scrap of paper. 'Have this! She gave it to me in her own handwriting.'

Liza said, 'But why are you doing this?'

'Because I don't like that woman. Any time she sees a young man with a girl, she will not rest till she snatch away the man from her.'

'Was Ricardo your man?' Liza asked. The girls eyes hardened. She spoke with hate in her voice.

'Yes... and then Kate Nene... she has no shame. No shame at all!'

'She took your man?'

'Listen . . . if I have time I can **tell** you about dat woman. She's a smuggler . . . proper one! Use to smuggle contraband from Cameroon . . . She smuggle gels too from over-side. I tell her say one day will be one day. 'With that she turned **and** wiggled back to the office switching her hips left to right. Liza watched her proud wiggle with interest.

Liza was able to trace the address in Balogun among a jumble of make-shift market stalls. Wedged in between a seller of wax prints and gold jewellery was a woman specialising in ready-made women's silk dresses mainly imported from Rome. When she heard why Liz had come she gazed at her with unconcealed suspicion.

She said. 'The owner of the stall done go home. She live at Ikeja.

Liza took the address at Ikeja and set off. She found the address she wanted in a compound off Awolowo Avenue.

She shoved at the iron gate set in a high wall. The gate yielded to her push. Across the compound she knocked at a half open door.

Liza pushed open the door and went in. She saw a shapely girl lying on a mattress spread on the lino-covered floor. Her hips arched where she lay, and when she turned, her eyes were large but sleepy. 'I'm tired,' she said. 'We sleep by one o'clock dis mornin . . .'

There were three other girls in the room, all of them of the same age, about eighteen or nineteen and all of them of the same height, between five feet two and five feet four inches. The one on the bed had tied

a piece of george cloth over her hard, orange-size
breasts. She had thick black hair and an ebony skin
which she exposed from the bosom upwards.

There was nowhere to sit. A fan was wafting the hot
air in the windowless room. Something about this
room reminded Liza of Auntie Kate's room in Jos,
and she concluded that Kate was still in the business
of providing girls for business executives.

'You are from Cameroons?' the sleepy girl said,
'You be Police or Customs?'

'No...I'll not hide matters. I am the step-
daughter of Kate Nene...Auntie Kate...'

'Ay-yah...' said the girl, almost tearful. She sat
up. 'Come sit down. Ay-yah...Kate never tell us she
get pickin' and a fine big woman too.'

She removed a few clothes from a chair and as Liza
sat, she rambled on. 'We don' know her movement.
She never tell us when she come and when she go...'
The other girls rolled over in various postures, all eyes
and ears.

'Even self, she use to come here when she get
market to sell and she go back to bring another new
market when she sell finish. Mostly she sell
contraband, and Customs People, you know them,
them worry her too much, so she use to take time,
make them no catch her.'

Now Liza began to guess why Alberto Ricardo was
so interested in Auntie Kate. The girl with the rich
hair frowned. 'Why you worry to see her so much?'

'I got a message for her,' said Liz.

'Try again day after tomorrow. You see, when she
come, she never sleep in this house, only in hotel or
with her man, that white man Ricardo.'

They heard the sound of a car outside. The car door banged, and footsteps sounded on the cement floor of the compound. Inside the room the four girls waited, tense.

There was a knock on the door. 'Come in!'

Liza recognised the caller as the man who had been with Auntie Kate at the lecture. 'Is Kate back?'

'No,' said Sleepy Gal.

She quickly slipped into a linen dress, made up her face, slipped on a pair of red shoes and followed Alberto Ricardo to his car, a Fiat.

Liza heard the car start and drive off.

'Foolish man!' said one of the girls. Whenever Auntie Kate travels he will sleep with anybody he see. As you see am so, two women no fit satisfy am. He like woman too much.'

'Auntie Kate keep us here. She say she will find work for we, no work, no husband, no boy frien'. I done tire self.'

True to his promise, Saka returned after midnight. The doorbell rang at precisely ten past one in the morning. Liza, groggy with sleep, checked the time and let him in.

'I just want to rest here tonight,' he said, and made for the bedroom.

'Feel at home.'

He did not report on the secret meeting, but she could sense that all was not well. She had been sensing that for some time. She knew his business was connected with shipping, forwarding, importing; and lately he had been talking about 'foreign partners' to set up some kind of manufacturing. She never pressed

114

him, he never asked for legal advice, and that was how it was.

She crawled into bed and he came and lay near her, snuggling closer and closer. Soon he was asleep.

When he opened his eyes it was after four. His first words were, 'Let's talk...'

'Now, what about?'

'About us.'

'I want to sleep.'

He began to complain. 'You do not take me seriously. I want you, and you think I'm joking.'

'Not true,' said Liza, suddenly awake. 'Not true, at all.'

'What's the position, then?'

'I don't want any more complications, Saka Jojo. My life has been full of it. Can you believe I don't know my mother, or my relations? Here I am with two children of different fathers, a trained and qualified lawyer with a Greek father, now deceased, a Nigerian mother somewhere at large, in short, an unsettled female. And you want me to join you, a big, busy businessman with three wives, plenty of money, no time for anything else but money...'

'Aa-ah!...'

'It's true. I'm sure, if you knew about me you would worry less about making me a 'wife' and be satisfied with things as they are.'

He smiled. 'What is there to know?'

'Okay, now you have me fully awake...Just imagine me as an eight-year old child, taken to England by my Greek father, Nick Papadopoulous and handed over to a British couple John and Barbara Thompson, old friends of my Dad who worked with him in Africa during the Colonial Administration?'

'There I completed Primary and Secondary School, bless the Thompsons. My father only came to see me when he was on leave. He always wanted me to be a lawyer and I am glad that I never disappointed him.'

Saka rose, went to the fridge and poured himself some whisky and soda. He sipped it slowly.

'You're drinking too much, Saka. You were smelling of alcohol when you came in.'

'It's nothing,' he said. 'What a good time to hear your life story.'

'When is there ever a good time, Saka Jojo, the Business Tycoon who is always commuting between Lagos and Tokyo, Brussels and Geneva, Amsterdam and London. When is there a good time? If you are going to call me your woman, you might as well know my history.'

'Okay, okay, no objection.' He waved the glass.

'Now where was I?'

'You were telling me about your father and the people you stayed with in England...'

'Yes...John Thompson had been in Sierra Leone before he married Barbara, fresh from Polytechnic where she had studied Fine Arts...I lived with them for nine years, and during that time I had developed into a young bosomy lass, ripe for love...I could tell by the way Thompson was always looking at me that his imagination was going wild over me. I could feel it and I was afraid. But we were never alone together. Barbara always managed to be around, even on working days. You never could tell when she would

116

barge in from art teaching on some flimsy excuse. I knew she was setting traps.

'John was not in regular employment. Sometimes he was home for three days at a stretch. He would remain in bed till his wife had left for school. He would be out in the afternoon, and in the evening, he would go to a pub.

'But, as fate would have it, one day, John and I were left together-alone. No visitors, no Barbara. I put on a coat and was about to step out.'

'Where you goin?'

'To the grocery.'

'Can't it wait?... Come here. Come, come here...'

I moved nearer.

He said, 'You're quite an attractive girl, you know that?'

I said nothing. He pulled me close and tried to kiss me. I turned my face away. He fussed all round me, pinching me, getting into a state. At the last moment, he was struggling with his zip when suddenly a convulsion shook his body and his tongue lolled out. I was scared, I thought he was having some kind of a stroke.

Then it was over and the sticky fluid had ruined his trousers. He moved away quietly towards the bathroom and I went out to the grocery.

From that moment on, I noticed he treated me with extra kindness, and once he called me and said, 'You woundn't mention it to Barbara would you?'

'What?'

'You know — what happened?'

'Oh, that! Forget it.'

It was about this time that I met Abdul Stevens from Sa Leone. Abdul used to tell me stories of West Africa. He was a law student also. I am sure it was he who influenced me to make up my mind to study law. We grew to love each other and when later I surrendered my virgin body to him, I knew nothing about the risk I was taking.

I felt all the signs without being able to understand them — nausea in the mornings, headaches sometimes, dizziness all of a sudden in the day time. Even when the child began cycling within my body I did not know what it was all about. There was no mother to guide me, and Mrs. Thompson regarded me more as a rival than as a friend.

You see, my father had sent me to England because from his knowledge of Nigeria, anyone who hoped to make a decent living must have a profession. He used to send them money and presents for me. Some of it they kept for themselves, and most times I never learnt about it till much later on.

In all those years, what I missed most was mother. If Auntie Kate was really mother why did I not see more of her? Whenever I asked my father he would tell me it was Auntie Kate. 'She does not want to come and live in England,' he used to tell me.

It was later on that I began to learn about little things — like racial prejudice. My father as a miner in Africa, could keep an African mistress in Africa for as long as he liked. Bringing her home to Greece was another matter. In the same way, as a daughter born of such liaison, it was best I was kept out of sight in some ways. And so John and Barbara Thompson were really doing my father a good turn, and he was prepared to endure a little inconvenience because he truly loved me. He used to tell me that I resembled his sister.

My father came on one of his visits.

'Liz, and how are you today?'

'I'm not feeling so fine.'

'That's unusual for my tough little girl.'

I smiled. 'Tough little girls are sometimes sick.'

'What's wrong?' his brow creased a little.

'I get headaches. I feel dizzy and I sometimes feel like vomiting.'

'The girl is pregnant', said Mrs. Thompson.

I looked up in surprise at the intrusion. 'Been meeting any boys? Come on, tell us the truth.'

I nodded.

'Who is it?'

'A law student, Abdul Stevens.'

'Well now... the one who brings you home sometimes?'

'Yes!' I had to admit the truth.

'You must go and see a doctor.'

I was sent to a National Health Doctor who referred me to a Gynaecologist and his report proved them correct.

'That night I overheard Mr. and Mrs. Thompson discussing me. I slept in the room next door.

'She has to go. Think of the scandal.' That was Barbara.

'No, darling. Anyone can make a mistake... and besides, they do these things in Africa.'

'What things? This is not Africa!'

'You've got to understand, Babs. You've lived

there yourself. The young man probably has four other wives.'

'Wait a minute, John. Are you telling me...'

'I'm telling you that the girl needs your love and care, this is why Nick sent her here in the first place.'

'To go sleeping around?'

'To be brought up by you.'

'Oh goodness! I knew you always had an eye on the wench. The number of times I've seen you pinching her bottom.'

'Darling!'

'Don't *darling* me. Think I don't see the look in your eyes when she wiggles her behind at you?'

'You mean I should stop having a beer or two?'

'It's not only when you're drunk that you lust after her, if that's what you mean...'

'So that's why you gave up Evening Classes — to keep an eye on...'

There was silence. I was feeling so very drowsy, and at the same time curious to know the conclusion.

'Anyway,' said Barbara, 'she has to leave.'

'You don't want to punish her for this first mistake... Listen Barbara, we have to take it easy for a while. Watch things. See how she makes out. Then...'

'Then we'll have a little brat screaming her head off nights, and I'll be the matron.'

'You've never liked her, because she is so downright sexy and gorgeous...'

'Well! You can have her anyday... I'll leave you two to your devices. I'm moving out in the morning.'

'Come on darling.'

I could hear her sobbing and John pleading with

120

her. She began to whine and cry aloud and he must have kissed her, then there was a struggle, I suppose they were making love. And then silence.

Next day, I showed no sign of having overheard the conversation, but I spent more of my time outside the Thompson's home, and began planning what to do with myself.

Abdul was shocked when he heard the news.

'I have only one room. Where will you stay?'

'I just want anywhere to stay until I deliver. I can hire digs, but suppose a fever grips me in the night? Who will phone the Ambulance?'

'What do I tell my people?'

'Nothing. They are three thousand miles away. I am not asking you to marry me, am I?'

'I don't want the child.'

'I do.'

'You can get an abortion.'

'No!'

'Christ! ... How did all this happen?'

'You were on heat, and as for me, it was all so strange...'

He helped himself to a straight shot of brandy.

'Why do you want the child?'

'Because I'm tired of being alone ... can't you see I am alone? My father keeps me here. My mother — who is my mother?'

'You told me Auntie Kate.'

'She's not. I discovered that.'

'Then who's your mother?'

'I'm still trying to find out. But meanwhile I want someone of my own. You can't take this child from me.'

'You're crazy, you hear?'

'Let it be so.'

'You're just damn crazy!' He hit me across the face. He hit me over and over till I could feel the blood in my mouth. I did not cry out. I was feeling aroused as he struck me, as I saw the glaze in his eye. Then he tore off my brassiere. My breasts were pimply and bouncy. He seized one of them in his mouth and began eating. I struggled and he threw me down and rode me till his madness spent itself. Then he stood up. He had not taken off his clothes. I lay there, feeling him moving about the bathroom. The front door banged and he was out in the snow. He did not come home until well in the morning, and then he lay in the three seater settee and slept off. I did not bother to go near him, for I was now feeling like a new bride full of control and power.

That was how I left the Thompson's. Throughout this time, Auntie Kate who claimed to be my mother, never once showed up. My father had gone back to the tin-mines in Jos and was back at work with the Consolidated Tin Mines of Nigeria. I wrote to him about it all and told him about my change of address.

I also wrote to Auntie Kate my supposed mother telling her about my plight.

One day I got a letter postmarked Nigeria, and looking closely I saw that it was from Jos. It was signed by Sister Heide. I knew she was illiterate so she must have paid someone to write it for her.

Dear Eliza,

I am your nurse who stays with Auntie Kate. I have to write this letter because I do not want you to suffer.

In my place when a young girl becomes pregant, she tells her mother. When she delivers, she sends for her mother. Auntie Kate is not your mother. Your real mother is a woman called Jagua Nan. She was a small girl, about your own age, when she was delivered of you. She hid the pregnancy. When she delivered she left you in care of Auntie Kate. I know because I was there. After, your mother ran from Jos for an unknown destination during the big riot at Jos between the Hausas and the Ibos. Many people were killed. Some were thrown into rivers and died there. By that time, Auntie Kate stole you and hid you somewhere.

When your mother came back Auntie Kate told her that you were dead, killed in the riot. She even took your mother to the graveyard where you were supposed to be buried. I was just looking at this wicked woman. May God forgive her. She will die in hell fire.

You may wonder why it has taken me so long to reveal this. The truth is that I am fed up with the woman. She thinks she will be young forever. She wanted your father to love, your father wanted her to produce a child, a boy, because he loved Nigeria and wanted someone to represent him here. You should be proud of your father indeed. He was a rascal as a young man, but very kind and loveable, very simple.

He was prepared to take any child from Auntie Kate Nene. Then one day Auntie Kate went to him and said, this is my child. She was using you to deceive Papadopoulous. Poor innocent man.

He died without knowing the truth. It was by accident that I got your address and am writing this letter to you in secret. Take care of your pregnancy. Do not worry. Do not abort the child and do not leave that child too long with anybody so that what happened to you may not happen to your own children.

I am sure God will bless you.

I am your Nanny.

Sister Heide.

I sat still for many moments after reading the letter. Then I began all over again, paying particular attention to various parts of it. I noticed that there was no address on the letter, and this made it impossible for me to reply. I remembered Sister Heide very well. It was she who loved me and mothered me as if I were her own child. Sister Heide had three children of her own and she had chosen to live with Auntie Kate at Jos, serving her all the time. She was not glamorous, like Auntie Kate, but she had a charming personality and attractive in a home-making way. I decided that the letter was genuine and sincere and the advice contained came from the heart. I made up my mind to do all the things Sister Heide had advised me to do.

But before that letter came, I was in correspondence with my father. In the CTMN the expatriate Senior Staff went on leave for six months out of every tour of eighteen months. Whenever my father came on his protracted leave, he always went first to Greece and once asked me to come over there for a fortnight.

Father used to tell me that I would turn out to be a beautiful woman, one of the most beautiful he had ever seen, and that he loved me and would never let me suffer.

When I asked him why he never married, he said he had had a bitter experience at the hands of a Greek girl whom he loved, and the shock of the disappointment as a young and ambitious man, had driven him into hunting and horse-riding and travel, finally settling down in Africa. It was during this visit to Greece that he showed me a picture of a certain very lovely woman with long hair down to her waist. Her name was Hilda, and father told me that she was his only sister.

I saw them often walking hand in hand like lovers. Their mother had died when they were both very young and they had been brought up as inseparables, with little distinction as to sex. Whenever I saw them like that, I was glad for him. After that visit, when his leave was over, he said he was going back to the tin-mines at Jos with Hilda, so that she might see Africa for the first time. He bought some guns and fishing gear which he said were for hunting and fishing.

Later on, he left the tin-mines and transferred to a gold-mining company on the upper reaches of the River Niger, near Sokoto, at a place called Malendo. There was a lot of game around this place at the time.

'I wish I could come with you,' I said.

'No, my dear. You stay here in England and study to become a lawyer. You can put your child in a nursery and concentrate on your studies.' His face darkened. 'I have made me all the arrangements. You will not suffer. No child of mine will suffer. You are all I have now — and of course, Hilda.'

Something about the way he talked made me panic. 'Daddy, I am afraid, Suppose you are — suppose you have an accident?'

'No...' His face was stern.

'But those guns you bought — are they **not** dangerous?'

'They're only sporting guns.'

'You talk about arrangements, and your face is dark.'

'Calm yourself, Liza... your Daddy will come back to you and will live to be 80.'

I laughed then, and a little lightness came into my life.

Hilda and my father set off for Lagos in a passenger boat called *Abosso* which travelled over the Bay of Biscay and Las Palmas to get to Apapa in thirteen nights. My father wrote to me at Las Palmas, then at Freetown, and after that, I did not receive any further letter from him.

I had forgotten all my forebodings about the guns and Africa and death.

But something troubled me. In one of his letters he told me that before he left Greece he made a will, leaving a substantial part of his property to me, on the condition that I be twenty-five years old or that I marry before then. He wrote, 'Something tells me that Kate Papadopoulous is not your mother. To the woman I believed must be your mother, your real mother, and who gave me so much happiness, I am also leaving something in case you ever find her.'

It was a very short letter and his last. With the arrival of Sister Heide's letter I was convinced that my father's suspicion was right. I found that indeed, Kate did not treat me with any tenderness, never expressed any fears for my safety. On the other hand, it was Sister Heide who troubled whenever I was out of sight or ill. It must be true that Auntie Kate was not my mother. It might also be true that because Kate placed so much emphasis on glamour, she would not want to be dirtied by a growing and dependent child. Either way, it was a worrrying thought.

It began to dawn on me that my father was a lonely man who had been disappointed by a Greek goddess, and who did not really believe in an African Queen. When later, I learnt that my father did not take Kate along with him to Malendo, I was not surprised.

Now some people said my father committed incest with his sister, Hilda, that is the bad gossip about him. The servants reported seeing them in bed together. They told this story to Auntie Kate who repeated it to Sister Heide. They said that at one point, Auntie Kate travelled all the way to Malendo, but was not well received and she left for Jos the very next day.

The story I heard about my father's death went something like this. You see, this gossip about incest finally reached him and he was very depressed.

He had a Winchester rifle, she had a double-barrelled Zabala shot-gun and she was said to be a good shot.

All this happened within six months of my father returning to Africa.

I was told that when they got into the bush they heard a sound, saw a swift movement. My father fired first and hit the animal but it ran into a thicket, which they surrounded. Hilda went to the other side. They were dead quiet in the bush for some time. Then a movement. My father fired in the general direction of

the movement. There was just one scream —
'Ohhh! . . . Nick you hit me!'

Father rushed and carried her in his arms and the
blood was pouring all over her silk shirt and below
her left breast.

She died in his arms. Nick Papadopolous let out a
loud cry.

'God, what shall I do? Whom shall I tell?'

He put the muzzle of the gun into his mouth and
fired. The hunting boys ran helter skelter into the
town shouting that the whiteman and his wife had
killed themselves. There was only one other
whiteman at Malendo at the time and he worked for
the United Africa Company at Sokoto. He sent down
a van to pick up the bodies.

That is the version of the story I know. I was very
much upset by all this misfortune and I could hardly
concentrate on my studies. There was no one to
advise me on how to handle all these complex life
problems, and I did not really care one way or the
other.

But one thing I decided: No man was going to fool
around with me.

'A great pity,' Saka Jojo said. He was silently
gazing at Liza with a new intensity.

'How was Obi born?' Saka Jojo broke the silence at
last.

I told you, there is something inside me that keeps
rushing when I see an attractive man.

He smiled. 'You are Jagua Nana's daughter
remember?'

I remember a school mate of mine once told me,
'Liza you are young, you are beautiful. You are

clever . . . what do you really want in life?' I replied
then that I didn't really know.

'Do you know now?' Saka asked.

'I'm beginning to. Africa has made me see the need
for family. I am sure I need to identify with my family
just as much as they need me.'

'When you say that, you look very serious.'

'Because I mean it' Liza said.

I met the father of Obi at a dance party organised
by the Commonwealth Union at Seymour Hall in
London. A gorgeous affair. Sumptuous hall, dazzling
lights, inspiring speeches about good relations
between Britain, Nigeria and the other countries in
the Commonwealth. Anti-apartheid sentiments.
There were some South African black students
present and they stood and cheered when a Lord who
was noted for his left-wing views said that Britain
should sever all links with South Africa — economic,
social and political.

At a point I noticed the way a Nigerian at the High
Table was looking at me, actually devouring me with
his eyes. I could tell he was a Nigerian by the way he
was dressed. He wore a dark jumper of *feni* cloth with
horses embroidered in dark brown, a black fez cap to
match, a bold necklace of coral beads hung on his
neck, and when he held up his glass to drink a toast,
the gold glittered on his fingers. He had good looks, a
flashy smile.

I had taken care to dress that evening. I was
wearing an off-the shoulder evening gown of
shimmering silk, my hair was pulled back from my
face, my eyes were well made up. I was in my prime
and I felt it.

Throughout the meal, he kept looking at me, to the point of rudeness. He did not smile. He had that cockiness you see in most Nigerian men who are young and have money. Like you, Saka. From the way people talked to him he appeared to be a man of substance.

After dinner the floor was cleared. I sat in a corner with some students. Two bands had come from Lagos specially to play for the occasion and as one of them began to play a juju beat I felt elated. I felt in my bones that I was a Nigerian to the core.

I had not been in Nigeria since I was eight years old because there was nobody to go to, nowhere to go. But that night brought Nigeria to me in London in a way that made me want to pack my things at once and set out for home. I felt the prickle of tears in my eyes and my nose began to drip though the room was quite warm. I brought out my Kleenex and wiped my nose.

My father had warned me not to return home, that I would suffer, unless I had some professional certificate. He was right. Nigerians I met told me that if I had a profession, life would be tolerable. At least I could stand on my own.

So I sat there and the music began to play and this man who had been staring at me all evening came close to me, bent down and asked me for a dance. I felt a strange vibration. I did not have to obtain permission from anyone else as I had come alone.

He told me he was staying at the Cumberland Hotel. Could I join him for a drink after the dance? I felt like Christmas, though something was warning me deep inside. I did not feel like going home. I stayed on at his table and the champagne sparkled and the corks popped and struck the ceiling, and I learnt he was a Nigerian business-man. He had an ocean liner of his own and ran a charter air service to the oil fields in Nigeria.

After the dinner and dance, we all went downstairs. He waved a hand and a black Rolls drove up, gleaming, and I felt like a princess as I stepped into the quiet inside. As he reached out and touched my knee, a tremor ran through me. It must have been the champagne, or the fizzy wine or the joy of it all. The bird inside me had fled its cage. I looked at him and saw the smouldering fire in his eyes.

Before we drew up in front of his hotel, he had kissed me, lightly, once. The chauffeur on the other side of the glass panel could have been a statue, though, knowing Englishmen, I could not swear he was unaware of what was going on. We were still locked in each others arms when he said, without turning his head, 'Ere we are sah!' And he came round to open the door.

I began to have romantic ideas about Nigeria, as a land populated by rich men who came to England to be served by white chauffeurs and stewards who take their money, plenty of it, say Sir' to make them feel big (and abuse them behind their backs for being extravagant and foolish). — not a romantic idea.

I slept at the hotel that night and became the mistress of George Nando. Each time he came to England, he brought me something from Nigeria, sometimes *Akwete* cloth or *adire* or some unusual food.

I began to explore parts of London to find the kind of food eaten in Nigeria and indeed there were shops

in England selling such food. It was a delight. Do you
know, he once persuaded me to come with him to
Lagos, and we flew in for the weekend and stayed at
the Victoria Beach, in Federal Palace Hotel.

Obi was born and Nando wanted me to abandon
all my studies and come home with him as his wife. I
would not do that. He said he wanted me to work in
his shipping company. I refused. I wanted to
complete my bar exams. We quarrelled.

I refused to give him custody of the tender child to
take away to some unknown step-mother. He said his
mother or grandmother would look after the child. I
told him no more step-mothers for me or my child if I
could help it. But his main concern was that this was a
male child and an heir. It was his first male child.
This seemed to be a disease among Nigerians —
having male children. 'Is it not still so?'

Saka looked at her but said nothing.

Jagua Nana's Daughter continued. 'It's all
forgotten now. When I graduated he came to the
convocation. Something was going wrong with his
business. He had been defrauded to the tune of
hundreds of thousands by one of his partners. He
looked wretched and dejected and my heart went out
to him. He wanted us to make up, for me to become
his wife. He did not mind if I remained in London as a
London wife. I thought about it for weeks. It was a good
offer. The man was young and ambitious and truly in
love with me. But I had this unfulfilled mission in life
— to find where I came from, to return home, to
understand my country.'

'That serious? Well, you're here now!' Saka
smiled.

'You may sneer at me but it's true. In the last few months in England, I was living in a flat of my own and dining at the Inns of Court.' Soon I was preparing to go home. I telephoned the Thompsons to say goodbye. It was Mr. Thompson himself who picked up the phone.

'It's Liza.'

'Oh, Liz, what a long time, and how're you?'

'Fine. Could I speak with your wife Barbara please.'

'She's out walking the dog.' He sounded as if he was happy she was not around.

'I might as well tell you — I'm returning home ... to Nigeria ... any time from now.

He did not seem to grasp it. This was a time when the Jamaicans and West Indians were flooding into London, "the mother country" looking for food and shelter and work. They came in shiploads, and we were told by the newspapers that at the other end it was one big business. And then in the midst of all that, for someone, a black person at that, to talk about returning home ...'

His voice came over low. 'I hear it's pretty rough out there. I hear they're now independent, and fighting like cats over plates of fish.'

'That's not Nigeria, that's the Congo!'

'Well, if it hasn't happened in Nigeria, it will, take my word for it ... It's all the same Africa!'

'British prejudice,' I said. 'Colour discrimination, colonial mentality.'

He laughed. 'Must you get back, Liz. How about ...?'

'Home sweet home.'

'You may be right. It might even be better to get out there and fight your way up.'

'If I can find the time, I want to come and thank you specially for looking after me as a kid. I'm a big woman now.'

'Our pleasure.' He sighed.

'A pity I failed your wife. I now have two kids of my own.'

'Really!'

'A boy and a girl.'

'How marvellous! From different fathers, no doubt' he sneered.

'You guessed right.'

Then it had occurred to Liza that if the Thompsons had any children of their own, they would be somewhere in India or Pakistan. They had never mentioned them even once during the nine years Liza was with them, and they had never visited.

'Will you send me a card from there?' She had noticed he did not say "us". His special secret desire for her was still there.

'I will, soon as I get there and settle down. But if I have the time while still here, I'll come in person. You were so good to me.'

'Good of you. Let's hear from you from time to time. And if ever there's a war, come back to Britain. It's always safer here, even in a World War.'

She laughed then. 'I shall remember that. If there's a war. Meanwhile, it's time to go home right now.'

For some reason I could not explain, the tears came rushing to my eyes. I took out a Kleenex, wiped my eyes and nose. When I put down the telephone I cried some more. It was not easy to leave Britain. At

134

a point I even asked myself, why all the fuss. Why not just stay there and make a home for yourself? What am I going back to Nigeria to do? Why, why, why . . .

In the short time since my father had died, the country had been rocked with fighting, rioting, burning and looting and every imaginable evil. The news from Nigeria as told in Britain seemed to be all about violence.

I was told that a part of the Cameroons from which my stepmother came had opted out of the Federation of Nigeria, while the other part, the Northern part, had opted in and become part of Nigeria, so we had a divided Cameroon.

My real mother, Jagua Nana, was still out there somewhere, known to Auntie Kate, but not to me. There was also the question of the will of my father and my need to belong to a family. No one ever told me whether my father had other wives or mistresses or whether he lived a single life and kept Auntie Kate as his only mistress.

My life stream was flowing in many directions. I was alone, and yet not truly alone. I needed my mother, I needed one man to call my own . . .

'That's me,' said Saka Jojo.

'Not quite . . .'

I also needed a home.

When I boarded the plane for home it was like leaving the known for the unknown. I had to tread warily. I was scared. That was when I met you on the plane. You were so kind to me, you did not mind the children. As soon as I set eyes on you I felt that spark I always feel about beautiful men.

Saka took up the story, 'Thank God for that engine

trouble. When our plane was diverted to Tripoli, and
we had to spend the night there, in a hotel, it was
heaven.'

'Oh yes.'

'Saka, my dear, what do you plan to do?'

'I want you to be my wife.'

'But it's impossible.'

'I don't have that word in my dictionary,' said
Saka.

'Do you ever see a dictionary? You're so busy
chasing after money.'

'So, now I've heard your story,' said Saka Jojo.

'And I'm happy about it.' Jagua's daughter leaned
back and watched him, waiting for his comment.

'It makes no difference to my desire.' He smiled.
'You see, life is full of ups and downs. My own story is
not better. I am the case of the street urchin who
made it big. I never forget that, and I thank Allah for
smiling on me. We just have to make the best of life
these days. Who am I to judge whether you are moral
or not? Let the elements do that. I am a mortal like
yourself.'

'So let's forget it. What time is it?'

'Nearly six in the morning.'

'What! I must be going. By the way, how was
Calabar?'

The case was adjourned. But there is something
else I noticed.

Saka turned sharply.

'The next war in Nigeria will start from border
disputes.'

'Why do you say that?'

'Go there and see for yourself!'

'The border is alive with fighting.'
'So?'
'Have you forgotten?'
'We were at the lecture together. Now I see that border clashes are not just idle talk. They are real . . . I was watching the local TV and suddenly there was this newsflash. Fighting has erupted on the border between Nigeria and Cameroons at a place on the Cross River . . . Come and see civilians carrying their belongings on their heads and fleeing! Some were moving into Cross River, some were moving back into the Cameroons. Confusion everywhere.

'That's serious, said Saka . . . And here in Lagos we don't even seem worried. Oh, well . . .'

'We'll just have to wait and see. What worries me is that a lot of those refugees are from the Eastern part of the country.

'Did you get any news about your mother's whereabouts?'

'No.'

Saka said, 'I have an idea . . . Why don't you set off one of these days. Go East.'

'I don't know the way.'

'Ask!'

'Go East and find that village mentioned in the letter . . . You might be lucky.'

'It's worth trying.' said Liza. And long after Saka had left, she kicked herself for not having made that move in the first place.

Chapter Seven

The Grandmother

From Onitsha Guest House, Jagua Nana's daughter
chartered a taxi and set off for the village of Ogabu.
They must have travelled for about an hour and she
must have dozed off. She opened her eyes when she
heard the driver asking, "Is this the way to Obi's
compound?'

She looked out and saw that the driver was
questioning a boy carrying a cane, one of a group
following a masquerade which had just disappeared
behind some banana leaves along a footpath leading
to a clump of houses.

The boy pointed to some palm trees in the distance
and the car moved off in the fading light. The un-
made road was well graded and the car showed no
signs of strain. They stopped before a bungalow.

'This is the place, I think,' said the taxi driver. He
opened the door for Liza to get down. Her high-
heeled shoes sank in the sandy soil. A curious crowd
started to gather from nowhere and they called her
oyibo, to her hearing. White woman. These constant
references to her skin colour were meant to be
complimentary, but they amused her.

She walked across the compound and climbed a
short flight of stairs to the landing. An elderly woman
opened the door and looked her up and down with
interest.

Liza felt uneasy.

'Am I in the house of David Obi, the preacher?'
'Yes'.
'Are you his wife?'
'You are asking these questions in peace?' the woman said, still fixing Liza with searching eyes.

Liza spoke in English. The woman listened carefully before she caught her meaning and gave her reply also in English.

'Pardon me, you speak like an English woman.'

'I was brought up there.'

The old woman sighed.

'My late husband could understand them well because he worked with many Reverend gentlemen, mainly Church of England ... He's dead now.'

Jagua's daughter moved closer. 'I have come home, mother.'

The old woman seemed to freeze where she stood, uncomprehending. By now the crowd was growing larger in the manner of crowds in villages that sense the imminent breaking of big news.

Liza said, and everyone heard her say it, 'I am the daughter of Jagua Nana, I am the lost daughter and I came here to look for my mother. I have been looking for her everywhere. They told me Ogabu is our village. I have never been here before. You must be my grandmother. Where is my mother?'

Jagua Nana's daughter paused, suddenly realising that the words were pouring out and that tears were filling her grandmother's eyes.

Grandma moved towards her and folded her in her arms.

'My daughter. Welcome home.'

She held her back and examined her for signs of

140

resemblance. 'Yes, now you say it . . . now I see the resemblance with my daughter Jagua.'

'God's work is great.' The crowd sighed. The news spread like harmattan fire. The oyibo woman is our daughter . . . Jagua Nana's daughter.

'Where did you come from? . . . England?'

'Lagos . . . Onitsha.'

'They said from the land of the white people.'

Ah! no wonder . . . she talks like them. She speaks in their language.

She looks and acts like them. Don't you see how she stands, with arms akimbo . . . See her straight nose! . . .

Liza beckoned to the taxi driver, asked someone to put down her things and paid him off. Her grandma, Martha Obi, Jagua's mother, led her into the house. The house was abustle with preparations. A fowl was chased, caught and killed. Yams were peeled and put on fire for pounding. Dried fish was washed, and pepper and onions ground. They were instructed to make pepper soup.

'This is how it was in the dream, back in London,' Liza told herself. 'It cannot be happening. That I am standing here in Africa, in Nigeria, in my very own village, among my own people.'

She sat down amidst the noise and the strange faces. Nick Papadopoulous, did he know this Ogabu? Grandma Martha sat opposite her. She took out a small tin of snuff and tapped on it. She took a pinch and sniffed and offered the tin to Liza. Liza shook her head and smiled.

'Did you pass through Onitsha?'

'No . . . What's in Onitsha?'

'Your uncle is there... Brother Fonso. He lives and trades in Onitsha Main Market. It is but one hour from here to his place.' She paused, looked her over and said, 'You cannot stay here. Why don't you go there and stay with him? You will be more comfortable.'

'I'm not after comfort,' Liza said. 'I want to stay here. I am your daughter. I must stay here. What! How can I tell people that I was unable to stay in my own village... What have I come for?'

Grandma said, 'But, how will you be comfortable? As for ourselves, we are used to the conditions. You are not... You should be staying at a good place like you're used to, and can be at ease. Here there's no shower...'

'But from what I see, its clean... That's what matters most... Never mind, Grandma. I have come here and that's all.'

Grandma sighed. She took Liza to her room. 'Your grandfather believed in one thing. Don't be a tennant forever. Always try and build your own place, however poor. Come with me.'

She led Liza into the compound. 'Here.' She pushed a door open. 'You bathe here.' There was a bucket of cool spring water, a sponge, toilet soap and a clean towel.

The WC was clean and spotless, no flies, signs of having been scrubbed that morning and disinfected too. Liza felt at the end of a journey.

Since she left Britain she had never felt so much at ease. Under one of the palm trees a young girl was pounding palm kernel. Liza went near and touched the oil, tasted it.

'She's making palm oil chop, very good for the body.'

'Shall we eat it tonight?' Liza said in her baby voice.

'If you so prefer' Grandma said.

Then Grandma began to talk about Jagua Nana. 'You resemble her in many ways... your shape, your eyes... the way you walk... But I'm sure you resemble your father more.'

Liza sighed and listened. Grandma told how Jagua had grown up at Jos, how her father David Obi wanted her to become a Reverend Sister in the Catholic Church and tried to send her to Convent School but she ran off, never studied. Always restless. She preferred to travel to the Gold Coast where she was called Jagua because of her shape and her love of fashionable clothes. 'After that I didn't know where she was. She just left home to find her way in life. Her father was disappointed in her and angry with her and until he died, he did not want to see her, but he prayed for her wherever she may be. He was heartbroken about her when he died because he loved her so much. She was our first and only daughter.'

Liza felt she had known her grandmother all her life.

'What does my mother look like? Tell me... I've never seen her.'

'Ah!... Jagua Nana? You will see her!' God created her. And she knows it too. Is it the hair on her head? Or the smile on her face? Or the way she walks and dresses? Or her shape, like something drawn by an artist. Your mother is not called Jagua for nothing.

Anyone who sees you, knows you are the image of
Jagua. Only the way I see you, you do not use your
body like your mother. You prefer to read books...
My daughter, since your mother grew up she has
been home only two or three times. I told you she
prefers city life. She travels a lot, that's why you will
not meet her here in Ogabu. She was here for the
memorial service of your Grandfather. She donated
money to the Church... No, she has not forgotten us
completely. She still remembers home.'

A noise coming from somewhere interrupted them.
Grandma rose and walked towards the front door.
Liza followed her. A disorderly group of people could
be seen pouring into the compound.

Liza gazed at Grandma in fear. 'Who are they?'

'Refugees,' said Grandma Obi. 'They are coming
from Cameroon. They are victims of the war on the
Cameroon's border...'

'War?'

'Yes, war. Soldiers and armed Police loot from one
town, burn houses on the border towns. The other
soldiers take their revenge.

'Is it that serious?'

Grandma said 'You are a witness now. Our people
go from here to work as labourers in the Cameroons.
Some have lived there twenty years. They intermarry
with the Cameroons people. They have children
there. That's how it is. But now, things are changing.
Excuse me, I want to go and talk to them.'

Grandma Martha descended the steps and went
among them. She raised her arm in salutation. The
wailing voice of a woman answered her. 'Help us! We
are suffering.'

A man held the woman and told her to be quiet. He explained to Grandma, 'They killed her husband. He went there to sell some things and was killed. Now she is a widow. There are so many widows day after day. What shall we do?'

From early afternoon the people of Ogabu began to assemble in the hall and spill into the village square.

The word has gone round the village that night, through the Town Crier, that a reception would be held for the returned daughter of late Catechist David Obi, Miss Elizabeth, who had been overseas most of her life. She was a lost soul, reclaimed. Everyone should endeavour to grace the occasion. *Gong! Gong! Gong!* intoned the *ogene*.

'Is all this fuss for me?' Liza asked.

Her grandmother touched her on the shoulder. 'My dear daughter your return is the will of God. We must give thanks to him. The people are happy.'

The secretary of the Reception Committee called at the Obi household several times to discuss the programme and eventually they agreed on something.

The traditional ruler of Ogabu was elected chairman of the occasion.

By four o'clock that afternoon, the village hall was packed full. Children were throwing and catching balls and darting here and there in their irrepressible manner.

Ezerioha 11, the *Okala Kala* of Ogabu arrived early and took his seat on the rostrum. He waved his leather and ostrich feathers fan in the still air while

lesser chiefs walked up to the high table, paid their
obeisance, whispered in his ear and took their seats at
the high table.

The formalities did not commence until five thirty
when at last, the MC rang a hand bell several times
and called the meeting to order.

There was silence.

'I greet you all.'

'Hem!'

'Ezerioha 11 the *Igwe Okala Kala* of Ogabu, I greet
you, Traditional Rulers, Administrators, our
daughter Elizabeth Obi, I greet you... We are
gathered here today to pay homage to lost-and-
found soul of our great village. People of Ogabu, God
loves us to the extent that Nene Elizabeth, traced
her way from overseas until she landed in this village
of her grandfather, without any help from anyone.
We are here to thank God for this, and so I call
upon *Igwe Okala Kala* 11 of Ogabu to lead us in prayer
and bless the kola nut.

Igwe Okala Kala rose with all ceremony. He said a
prayer in the Christian manner to which the reply
was 'Amen', and then he lifted the calabash of kola
nuts and began to call upon his ancestors amidst
intense silence.

'Long Life... That's what we ask you, Endless One
above, without a beginning or an end, we seek your
protection for our daughter, we pray you grant her
the wisdom of the ages, so that she might reap from
both worlds. Her real father was a white man, a Greek
named Papadopoulous, may his soul rest in peace...
he has moved on and left her behind for us. Have no
fear, our gods shall protect and guide you in all you

146

do. Earth does not refuse its sustenance. You are one of us and will always be.'

Liza fanned her face with a raffia-knit fan. She was dressed in a heavy hand-woven material given to her by her grandmother. Two rows of beads adorned her neck. Everything she wore smelt of camphor. Grandma Obi had explained that they had to put camphor to keep away insects. It was the old way. On Elizabeth's head was wound a headtie of heavy woven cloth in blue and beige. When she walked in her high heels, the solid earth responded.

Grandma said, 'You are a thing of beauty, a delight to the eyes. God bless you.'

After the speeches, refreshments were served. And then the introductions. This is your brother... That is your uncle... This woman is our sister on the father side... Faces appeared before her in flashed animation. She was amazed that all this did not bore her, that her smile was genuine and warm. She kept reminding herself. These are my people. I travelled long distances to see them... from now on, no one will dare call me rootless.

A woman asked her a question in Igbo and it was interpreted to her.

'She wants to know where your children are.'

'Tell her they are in Lagos.'

It was translated.

'Why did you not bring them?'

Again, translated.

'I'll do so next time I come here.'

'We expect you... they must come to know their home.'

'You are right... what you say is correct.'

The woman moved on and entered the crowd, her point well taken.

The dancing began, then the masquerade came. Liza noticed that the women began to disperse in haste. Masquerades are not formed for women...

As darkness came, Ezerioha 11 *Egwe Okala Kala* of Ogabu and entourage departed. Grandma Martha Obi said, 'Get up and greet them, they are leaving. And Jagua Nana's daughter got up went towards them and curtsied.

'I wish your grandfather David Obi was here... To see you with his own eyes... and your mother... where is she?'

He spoke excellent English. He had served in many roles in the Public Service before coming home to help his people.

'I am still searching for her,' said Liza.

'You will see her — soon, I'm sure.'

She curtsied again. The entourage flowed slowly out and was swallowed by the tall trees across the open field.

More dancing and drinking followed, but this part of the ceremony was for the less privileged who cared little about decorum as long as there was food and drink. The chairman of the occasion had departed and with him went the heart of the matter.

Jagua Nana's daughter and her grandmother got up to leave.

In the night Liza could not sleep. The air was still and the mosquitoes buzzed. There was the sound of a solitary owl coming from the church graveyard. She went and sat in the sitting room and Jagua's mother came up to her.

'My child, you are restless. What are your plans?'

'To visit Brother Fonso in Onitsha.'

'And then?'

'I must go back to business. My partners will be worried about my whereabouts.'

'You have known where your mother comes from ... and your grandparents too ... but this is not a proper visit ... you must come back with your children. I want to know them.' She fell silent suddenly.

After a while she spoke slowly to herself.

'Do you know? I have become a great-grandmother. But until I see your children with my own eyes, I shall not believe it's true ... how many people can live to be a great-grandmother in these times? You see ... we have longevity in our family, And this you know. It is your inheritance.'

Jagua Nana's daughter said, 'I'm glad.' Her heart was full.

'Tell me about your father,' said her grandmother.

Liza looked up and said, 'Nick Papadopoulous ... a very handsome man. He comes from Greece. He lived and died in Nigeria. He was really a Nigerian. He drank the local beer and he had a Nigerian mistress Auntie Kate, but Kate was not fertile, and he wanted a child from her. So she planted my mother and I was conceived and after that, she played her game so well, that I believe my father died without knowing that I was not born by Auntie Kate. In fact, until recently, I myself did not know she was not my mother. It is very upsetting.'

'What! What are you telling me?'

'Grandma, I am telling you that Auntie Kate made a wicked plan against my mother. Because of that my mother suffered a lot and vowed to avenge her.' Grandma wrung her hands in anguish. 'In the name of God, do not do anything wicked to her. She has erred, but you should forget...'

'It will depend, Grandma. She was too callous.'

'This Nick Papadopoulous, he lived in Jos?'

'Not in Jos... in the tin mines behind the rocks of Jos. I was too small to know it well. But I remember him.'

Jagua's mother thought a little... 'I seem to remember... I did not know him... myself and your grandfather lived in Jos at the time... we used to watch some white men come along in their pick-up van to some women just across the road... So that is how it happened. And I never knew my poor daughter Jagua was mixing with them!'

'You know my father died?' Liza said.

'How could I?'

'He died... it was a hunting accident. He shot his sister in the bush...'

'What?'

'They were in the bush together. They saw an animal... she pursued it. They surrounded the animal. Father saw a movement and fired, not knowing it was *NOT* an animal but his own sister. She had come all the way from Greece only to be shot in Africa. My father was heartbroken. He put the muzzle of his gun in his mouth and pulled the trigger... That is how it happened. The two of them were buried in Malendo, the place they said he died. It is terrible indeed.'

'It is God's wish, my daughter. Bear it like that. What has happened has happened. I am indeed full of grief.'

Liza drew comfort from the deep concern of her grandmother.

When they finally turned in, she slept till morning when a maid woke her. She had never slept so deeply since she returned from England.

'Your grandfather's brother,' said Grandma.

'Where is he?'

'In the parlour, waiting to take you to his place.'

'Where is that?'

'Here in the village... It is part of your home-coming. Get ready and follow him.'

Jagua's daughter put on slippers and slacks and came into the parlour to meet a grey-haired man whose face was clean-shaven. His eyes were grey and moist and he stared at Jagua's daughter with undisguised lust.

Liza greeted him.

'Are you ready?'

'Where are we going?'

'Just follow me.'

He lived not very far away. They passed along a narrow path between a row of houses and into a compound where a goat was tethered to a shrub. He led her across the verandah into a darkened room and sat her down. He himself sat opposite her on a leather skin and before him was a flat patch of sand.

As her eyes grew accustomed to dim light, she began to discern the wierd decorations on the wall. Skulls of animals, skins, fiercely-grinning masks. The room smelt close and tight.

He paid no attention to her but busied himself with chanting incantations. After a while he paused and began to throw cowrie shells on the sand and arrange them in patterns.

'Touch my hand,' he said, extending his calloused palm for her to touch. He made an imprint of her touch on the sand and continued with his incantations.

Then he began to speak. 'You are troubled with the world... You do not know where you belong... But take heart, all will come right. You shall find a husband who will love you, and relations, many of them. You have returned home and you have been long overdue. But there are evil forces. If you ignore them, death will be the consequence. I shall give you something, but meantime, you must strip and let me anoint you with a protection.'

Out of curiosity, Jagua Nana's daughter stripped. He produced sharp-smelling ointment from under his seat and began to anoint her body. He took special delight in anointing her breasts, lingering on each one, massaging and running his hard fingers over them one by one until Jagua Nana's daughter began to feel aroused, then he turned her round and massaged the small of her back and down to the cheeks of her bottom, and suddenly his hands found their way between her legs, but briefly, and then down to her calves and he was done, mumbling all the while.

'Do not wash this off till morning. Put on your clothes. You have come home indeed.'

He produced a powder in a paper and a small bottle containing a dark liquid.

'Sprinkle a little in water before you bath. Rub the liquid as I have shown you — before you go out and meet the world. Our ancestor's spirit shall guide you.'

'Your grandfather did not believe in *Juju*', said Ma Jagua. He went with the Christians and joined them to destroy the oracles and other things. But Bart has always worshipped demons. Nothing can change that. It is a good thing you went to see him. If you were not a relation, that treatment would cost you a lot of money. Many of his children are English-trained doctors and lawyers, and it was from this practice that he paid their fees. He has seldom left Ogabu, except when people from afar send for him, and then he spends only few days.'

In the morning, as Jagua's daughter prepared to leave for Onitsha, she noticed a lorry standing in the driveway.

'They have just come back from Cameroon with the dead,' said a passer-by. 'It is like this now every-day.'

Later on, Liza learnt that one of the dead was the last brother of David Obi who had gone to Cameroon in his youth and had made good there.

'This business is coming nearer home,' said Grandma Jagua. 'We are praying to God to spare our lives.'

'Grandma, is this how it is?' Liza said. 'Who is fighting their case?'

'My daughter, nobody,' said Grandma. She sighed. We are left with the burden of the dead.'

'It is bad... Someone should do something. Yes! When I get to Lagos...'

Grandma placed a restraining hand on Liza's shoulder. 'It is a very big matter indeed. Don't put yourself into it.'

'We shall see,' said Liza.

She embraced Grandma and just before entering the taxi, Grandma reminded her, 'Don't forget to call on Brother Fonso.'

Chapter Eight

The Meeting

Liza yawned, stretched and got out of bed in the Onitsha Catering Rest House. She did not feel like going down to Brother Fonso in Onitsha Market Road for lunch. She had made no formal appointment with brother Fonso and his wife, Stella, though she knew they might be expecting her. She hoped they would not be too offended if she failed to show up.

She strolled to the dining salon and chose a table in the far corner. From here she commanded a good view of the entrance and beyond it between the trees, she could just catch a glimpse of the River Niger, a broad silver glimmer in the distance, reflecting the light of the sun when it moved out of the clouds. There it was, flowing ever so imperceptibly towards the delta, a sight to soothe the nerves.

'What will you have Madam?'

A waiter had appeared at her elbow.

'What do you offer?'

'Roast beef, Sirloin steak, Nigerian dish.'

'What Nigerian dish?'

'Pounded yam with *egusi* stew.'

'Is that all?'

'*Amala* with *ewedu* and fresh fish from the river.'

'No okro soup?'

'You mix it with ewedu, Madam.'

While they were bantering and haggling, Liza saw

the entrance darken and a magnificent-looking couple pause at the entrance, scanning the scantily populated dining room from one side to the other.

The woman was tall, big bosomed, shapely and fashionable. Liza felt that sudden flash of recognition which had stunned her on the night she first saw Auntie Kate at the Institute of International Affairs lecture. A pulse began to throb in her head.

This woman would be about the same generation as Auntie Kate, but looked much younger, with more spring in her all round. She had the same regal presence, and though Liza could not see the eyes behind the dark glasses, she felt the x-ray intensity of her searching gaze. The man attracted her attention by his splendid physique and casual elegance. The open-necked shirt showed a gold chain nestling in a bush of hair, which was reflected in the high pile of Afro hair on his head.

In that brief moment Liza's glance was riveted on the woman as if each of them wanted to speak, then she moved on, followed by the man, and the moment was lost.

They took a table situated so that Liza could not lift her eyes without meeting that commanding gaze of the woman. The more Liza looked, the more restless she became. Something about that woman came across to her with living force. She felt a headache coming.

She placed her order and waited to be served. A waiter moved to the other table. She saw the waiter bend his head while the woman whispered in his ear.

As she watched, the waiter came towards her.

'Madam,' he said, 'They ask if you can join them?'

156

'Is that so?' Liza felt like a loose woman being picked up. 'But I don't know them!'

'They want to know you...' He moved with precision. 'Let me take you there.'

Liza followed the waiter, stepping gingerly between the tables until she got there and stood rather awkwardly.

They exchanged greetings.

The woman said to Liza, 'I feel I know you, please do not be angry wit me. Someting inside me push me to do dis. I just feel I know you.'

'Maybe,' said Liza in a distant voice. 'But I do not live here in Onitsha...'

'We too... We arrive last night — from Jos.'

'Welcome' said Liza, still rather suspicious.

The woman made a swift pass over her face and the dark glasses came off.

'Jagua Nana, das me... And dis my man — Tobias Moma... Hotel man of Akwanga.'

'What!... 'Liza screamed before she knew it. My mother!'

Jagua said, 'Eheh!... I knew it! Blood smells. I smelt you, my daughter. Come to me!'

Liza leapt into her mother's arms scattering the well-laid table. They folded each other tight, rocking from one side to the other like playful wrestlers, to the consternation of the arriving guests.

The stewards looked on, perplexed.

'*Chineke*!' exclaimed Jagua, 'All my suffer finish! No more! I get a daughter like dis, what more?'

Tobias Momoh stood like a referee who wants to shout 'foul' as two champions grapple. The smile on his face was a thin veil over his anxiety.

Finally he separated them. 'Why, you two are crying!' . . . Handkerchiefs came out and mother and daughter wiped their tears, then began crying all over again.

Jagua kept saying, 'My sufferness done end, my sufferness done end. I fit die, now, I no mind. Oh God, I tank you. You keep my life reach dis blessed day!'

They talked about Auntie Kate, and Liza revealed how she had sighted her at the Cameroons Embassy Cocktail Party and how Auntie Kate had fled with her escort, one Alberto Ricardo, a construction man, and how she had traced Auntie Kate to a place in Ikeja where she kept sex-slave girls. Since then she had lost her.

'But what you want see her for?'

'You tink if I saw her I wouldn't kill her after what she has done to me?'

Tobias looked on confused.

Then Jagua explained to him in Ibo that this young lady here was born in Jos. 'I was a small girl den, seventeen years. I did not know dat Auntie Kate tief dis girl, and say is her daughter. She told de white man who keep her, dat is Nick Papadopoulous, and Nick love her more and give her everything she want. Dats all-o! I never see my daughter since. But I begin to hear de story small small.'

'It got to me, too,' said Liza.

Tobias said 'It must. How can you hide a thing like that.'

'Elizabeth, my daughter "God bless you."'

The tears began to come again, and they knew that for them, eating their lunch was out of the question for the afternoon.

It was Tobias Momoh who directed the stewards to move everything over to their rooms where they could talk undisturbed.

Liza came down early next morning and was waiting in the dining room when Tobias and her mother joined her. She rose, smiling and embraced her mother. The glow of pleasure never once left her, nor did she fail to admire the couple, especially her mother. I wish I would grow into such a lovely lady, she thought.

Tobias sat down and ordered corn flakes, bacon, liver, sausages and coffee. Jagua ordered the same.

Liza said, 'Is that how you eat? I'll have toast and marmalade and coffee.'

Tobias smiled. 'Let dem serve me for a change.' There was a mischievious glint in his eye. 'A hotelier deserves some break sometime. Maybe the demolition of my hotel is a good sign.'

Jagua held her hand. 'I tenk God,' she said, looking with admiration at Liza. 'As I see you now, my own daughter wit my own eyes. I fit die now, I never mind.' She turned to Tobias. 'We will reach Ogabu today.'

'Liza, you will come with us, after we see Brother Fonso.'

During breakfast Tobias told Liza about Akwanga. 'The business was good. It started simple. I was all alone. I cleared the bush, built eating houses, then sleeping houses. I made a big space for lorries and cars to park, mechanic shed, petrol station, everything ... Soon, some other people begin to join me, until all those trailer drivers take the place as

159

their place for rest on the way going North or returning South. When you reach there, you can go to Jos or Abuja or Kaduna, or you can go South to Benue and Garua. Is a very central place, but I am the man who made the place, Travellers Inn.'

He shoved a large spoonful of cornflakes into his mouth. When your mother joined me, the business multiplied ...

'Tobias is a good man', said Jagua.

'Your mother is a wonderful lady. Anybody who speaks bad of her, I will kill him with my two hands'. As he said this, his eyes flashed. For a moment, Liza noticed the steely determination in the set of his lips.

'No need to kill anyone,' Liza said.

'People talk a lot of bad about someone they don't know. If you know this woman, you won't want to know anybody else. Jagua Nana is a kind woman.'

'You mind dem? So-so back-bite for dis worl' said Jagua.

'This Jagua did them nothin' said Tobias. 'They're just jealous.'

'Wait,' said Liza 'Just take it easy. I can see you love Mama so much.'

'She's not Mama to me. No sixteen year old gel fine pass her. And she get too much sense.'

They ate in silence.

'We will go and see your Grandma togedder ... and den — I want Ma to see me, Jagua Nana and my Bebe Jagua togedder! she liked the idea of calling her daughter 'Baby'. It made her feel good.

'I'm just from Ogabu. "Good girl"' said Jagua.

'Now,' said Liza 'I want to return to my work in Lagos.' She told her mother about the search for

160

Auntie Kate and how she had narrowed it down to Balogun and Ikeja. The Cameroons Embassy was also helpful. 'There is a girl in that Embassy who is always helping me.'

'I want to face dat Auntie Kate' said Jagua.

'Leave it all to me.' Liza begged.

'Is too late,' said Jagua, 'I already gone too far.'

'I want to know a little more about my father,' said Liza.

Jagua said, 'Anodder time . . . Dat wicked woman! You think she will tell you? . . . Dat selfish woman . . . ?'

Tobias excused himself. 'We have to check out.' He went over to pay the bill.

Jagua watched him. 'Since I be small gel, I never have rest of min' wit any man like Tobias.'

'He likes you too, I can see that.'

'Now' said Jagua, 'so you will stay in Lagos?'

'Yes.'

'What about husband?'

'No plans yet.'

'You have no man? Don't be like me.'

'I have one man.'

'From where.'

'He's a Lagos businessman. His name is Saka Jojo.'

'Businessmen used to disappoint. Just take care, dats all. Why you no marry him and settle down?'

'He already asked me.'

'And you refused?'

'No.'

'You agreed?'

'No.'

Jagua shook her head. 'So?'

'I'm still thinking. You see, Ma, I have two
children. He does not mind that., But he has three
wives. We are lovers. He visits me... the
arrangement is good — so far.'

'Oh! Daughter of Jagua!' She laughed. 'I remember
myself, is like dat, Liza. God bless you, you're such a
beautiful woman any man will run mad for you.'

'Mama, I searched and searched for you and now
you're here, I don't know what to do.'

'Dere is noting to do. Just rejoice and tenk God.'

In the evening they trooped into Tobias Range Rover
and set out for Ogabu. Grandma Jagua danced with
joy. 'Now I can die' she said. 'Jagua, you look after
them! I'm going to pray and sleep.'

Tobias and Jagua were still asleep in their room
next morning when Liza knocked at their door.
'Mama, there is a beautiful girl just arrived. She says
from Krinameh. She wants to see you.'

'Where's she?'

'In the Parlour.'

'Did she give a name?'

'Tamuno.'

Jagua leapt from the bed.

'Tamuno! Dat junior wife to Chief Ofubara. What
she want?'

'I don't know. Didn't ask her.'

Tamuno rose as Jagua Nana entered. She looked
taller, slimmer, more sophisticated. She wore a green
and black patterned accra dress, well cut and slim-
fitted. The blouse and wrapper, headtie, matched.
She did not smile.

'Mornin.'

'Mornin, Tamuno. I lef Chief Ofubara for you.
Why you follow me come here for?'

Tamuno sat down. 'Are you surprise to see me?'

'Yes. Who show you de way?'

'I ask people. They direct me.' She coughed lightly
and seemed uneasy. Jagua said, 'How's Chief
Ofubara, your husband?'

'He died,' said Tamuno. 'That's why I come here.'

At first the words did not register.

Tamuno went on. 'He said they should not bury
him till you come. He was calling your name when he
died. Where is Jagua? Don't bury me till I see her.'

'You make me fear,' said Jagua and she began to
weep.

At that moment, Tobias and Liza entered the
sitting room.

Tamuno greeted them.

Liza said, 'You must be hungry. Let me get you
something to eat.'

Jagua introduced them.

'Tamuno, dis is my daughter, Liza. I fin' her at
last!'

Tamuno rose and stretched out her hand. 'You born
pickin wey big like this? And she's so beautiful!'

'And dis is my husband' said Jagua.

Tobias stretched out a hairy hand. Tamuno looked
deep into his eyes and for a moment they both
regarded each other with undisguised interest.

Jagua said to Tobias, 'Dis is de wife of Chief
Ofubara of Krinameh in the Rivers. De man wanted
to marry me. Dis is de junior wife ... Tamuno. Tank
God, she did not let de Chief marry me. I for no meet
my man Tobias.'

'All that be past tense,' said Tamuno. There was a new seriousness in her behaviour.

'Tamuno just bring me news dat Chief done die and dem want me to go to Krinameh, or else dey will not bury am.'

'We will go together,' said Tobias with decision. 'When?'

'Is it far?'

'From here to Port Harcourt is not far. But after Port Harcourt is two hours by outboard engine canoe.'

'It's morning now ... we can go at once,' said Tobias when he heard the details.

Tamuno said, 'I am not coming with you. I have an Auntie in Lagos I want to see, I cannot go back to Krinameh again.'

'A pity,' said Jagua. 'But why not? so now dat Chief die, you run away?'

'Is not so. I have no place in his house. I have no child for him!' She burst into tears and Jagua took her in her arms and let her cry.

Liza said, 'Mother, I have to be back in Lagos. Will you be coming later?'

'I must come and know how you live dere!'

'I shall expect you.'

Tamuno said. 'Take me wit you to Lagos!'

Liza considered.

Jagua said, 'Take her. She never see de worl'.'

'I like you,' said Tamuno, looking at Liza. 'I beg you to take me.'

'I feel sorry for you,' said Jagua, and Tamuno wept louder.

'But you jealous too much, you wicked too much

164

and now it's all in vain. De Chief die.'

Tamuno broke into sobs. Her shoulders shivered. 'I feared you. I did not want you to take away my Chief. But now the Lord done take him.' She began to sing.

'Forgive me . . . forgive a foolish gel. It was love. That's how it is.'

'So you loved that ol' man?'

Everywhere was quiet. Liza stood at the door watching her mother dry the tears of Tamuno. Tobias tried to hurry them up.

We must set out now for Port Harcourt so we can get there before darkness comes, if we don't reach Port Harcourt in good time, we cannot cross tonight and reach Krinameh. We must be back tomorrow.

'I'll be in Lagos then.'

'One moment,' said Tobias and he took Liza aside.

'I have been talking to your mother, he said. I want to start up again. I have a little money.'

'What do you want to do?'

'The same thing . . . hotel business, but this time on the Benin Expressway, in a completely new place, just like the one at Akwanga.'

'How do I come in?' Liza asked.

'You will help with formalities, registering the company. Call it JAGUA NANA ENTERPRISES LTD. Yes, your mother is lucky. I want to use her name. We shall run a hotel for travellers, big open field for parking trailers and lorries, chicken farm for eggs and meat. Cassava for garri. That road is swampy. If we get occupancy for a swampy area, then it will be rice.'

'Rice no dey grow dere,' said Jagua, eavesdropping.

'Wetin dey gro dere?'

'Plantain,' said Jagua.

'You're right, you know'. He turned triumphantly to Liza. 'Your Mama is a great woman. Bless her.'

He held her hand and said, 'Go and get ready.'

Liza said. 'Tamuno, come with me. Lets bid Grandma goodbye.'

Tobias smiled. 'If this business succeeds, I shall make you a special chalet where you can be coming to rest from Lagos worries.'

'You must succeed,' said Liza, 'God willing!'

Chapter Nine

The Wives

Liza parked the Honda outside her residence. Suddenly she had that strange feeling, that invisible eyes were probing her every move. She felt, that she saw the neighbours standing behind curtains at the windows watching something. As a general rule she tried to keep out of the urban curiosity that Lagos dwellers had for spectacle, the more violent, the more entertaining. She reminded herself that whatever it was, her maid Titi would give her the details.

Then she saw Titi running towards her and was startled.

'Madam, some . . . some people are looking for you!'

'Who are they?' Liza tried to be cool.

'Ah don' know dem, Ma. Dem begin make trouble with Madam Tamuno. Three of dem, all women. Ah never see dem before.'

'Tamuno?'

'Dem hold her and tear her dress. Dem tell am to talk where you hide yourself.'

'Tamuno, for goodness sake!'

Liza hurriedly locked the car, leaving her groceries inside. She began to blame herself for yielding to Tamuno's eloquent pleading to take her along with her to Lagos from Ogabu. She had claimed that she wanted to get away from Krinameh, that she wanted to go to Lagos to seek her fortune, that she had an

Auntie in Lagos. But Tamuno had stayed on with Liza and Liza had grown to like her, she was so serviceable, such a good companion.

Liza's first instinct was to call for immediate help, but she held back when she remembered her two children and instead hurried towards the house, Titi trailing beside her.

'What about Ngozi and Obi. Eh, Titi? Are they safe?'

'I keep dem in de room, but dey are crying for mummy.'

'What did the strangers say?'

'Dem talk about dem husband, dem say he used to follow you too much.'

Titi's words gave Liza the clue and she suddenly understood. This was the moment that must come. She took a deep breath and decided to face the matter squarely. She walked straight into her sitting room. She looked round. Three women stood tense, glowering at her. There were no introductions.

One of the women sprang forward and began to rain abuses at Liza. Another one pretended to calm the spokeswoman down and said, 'Wait — let us talk to her. She's a woman like we are.'

'Madam, what is your business with our husband Saka?' asked the one who appeared to be their leader.

'Business? What do you mean,' Liza asked.

'We mean that you steal our man from us.'

'Nonsense!'

Liza felt the high tension. At a glance, she saw Saka Jojo's taste in women. One was tall and delicate looking. The one who appeared to be their leader was heavy-breasted with big arms, obviously the Madam.

168

The third one, like Liza was a cross-breed. She had European hair and a fair skin.

Tamuno came across from one end of the sitting-room and stood beside Liza.

'Don't mind them,' she said under her breath. 'If they want trouble, we give it to them. Why can't they hold their man? Is it your fault Saka is mad after you?'

Aloud she said, 'Go put chain round your husband!'

'You — shut up! Harlot!'

They stood glaring at Liza and Tamuno. The tall delicate-looking one removed her headtie and knotted it around her waist. This was clear signal for physical combat.

Suddenly something flew across the room and hit Liza on the forehead. She cried out in pain. Stars danced before her eyes. She looked down, picked up the wooden carving of an elephant and hurled it straight back at the elegant cross-breed woman. It missed its target and crashed into a mirror, shattering it to pieces.

Next moment, the room had become a battle-ground. Dresses were rent asunder, hair was pulled out by its roots, pale complexions were scratched.

'They bite me!' cried Tamuno.

'Have you no teeth? Bite them!'

Liza and Titi reached out and seized broom handles and a chair, and swished them down on the back of the neck of the big shapely woman who was converging on Jagua Nana's daughter. She staggered and fell, picked herself up and ran. The others followed suit.

The neighbours were pounding on the front door, but the wives had made their escape through the back door, dishevelled, wigs scattered on the floor, brassier straps broken. They fled to the safety of Saka's Mercedes 500 SEL. The elegant cross-breed wife was at the wheel, her face now red and swollen. The others piled in and with a screech of tyres, the sports car spun away amidst curses from neighbours who wanted to know what the fight was all about.

They learnt nothing.

Jagua Nana's daughter stood before the mirror examining her torn dress and swollen eyes and lips. She felt humiliated and angry. Saka Jojo should be here to see the damage done to her person and her property by his wives. She asked herself whether it was worth it, to be the mistress of a man with three wives.

'Is a good ting if you can put dem all in prison,' said Tamuno.

'Saka will not like it,' Liza said.

Tamuno was turning round and round like a model, examining the split in her dress right down her back. On her throat were teeth marks.

'What do you care what Saka likes? Because he's your man is that why?'

'He's taking too long.'

'Maybe, some emergency,' said Tamuno. 'Has he returned from overseas trip?'

'He did not tell me about it,' said Liza. 'But I'm sure he's abroad. He would have been here.'

Titi brought in a bowl of hot water with a towel and some balm. Tamuno took the towel, soaked it in the water, wrung it and pressed it against Liza's eyes.

170

'Ouch!'

'Is paining you?' Tamuno asked. 'Have patience... You will be wearing dark glasses for some time. Your eyes are swollen.'

Next morning, Liza called at the GOOD HEALTH CLINIC at the corner of the road and complained of pains in the ribs and back.

Tamuno said her eyes hurt, and the tummy felt as if it had been pounded with a pestle. The Doctor wrote a comprehensive report. Liza took a copy.

They were given prescribed tablets and injections on the bare buttocks by the Pharmacist and told to report next day.

Throughout all this, Liza thought seriously about Saka Jojo. There was no sign of him, and no explanation. She decided she would not call at SAKA JOJO GROUP OF COMPANIES in Broad Street to inquire about him. Never had her spirits sunk so low since she decided to come home to Nigeria. If this was the way Saka Jojo would abandon her in moments of need then he was not man enough for her.

When she called again at the Clinic the next day, she was told after examination by the doctor that they would each have to take a bed for a number of days to undergo tests and observations.

'Hope nothin very serious,' said Titi, when Liza informed her she would be at the Clinic.

'Nothing...'

'They will let me see you?'

'Why not?'

Titi's face brightened.

The next few days crawled by. Nothing much happened.

Then Titi reported that there were two visitors at home, but one came direct to the hospital.

To her surprise one afternoon, she was told that a visitor was coming to her bed. He came in quietly and Liza, gazing at his face could hardly tell who he was.

'I am Judge Macros,' he said.

She sat up sharply in her bed.

'Your Lordship...'

'The Doctor who runs the Clinic is a close relation of mine. He told me you were ill, and...'

'It's very kind of you.'

He presented her with flowers.

He sat beside the bed for a while, then left.

Tamuno smiled. 'The man likes you.'

'He's an old man,' said Liza.

'Old men are the best. They have experience, they are kind, not rough like the young ones. They are responsible.'

'It's just a visit.'

'Ah...'

'You think there's something in it?'

'I watched the man's face, I see everything there. The man likes you. He get wife?'

'Judge Macros ... his wife died about two years now. Very famous woman. Worked with the Red Cross and some Voluntary Organisation. I hear the man is very strict, a disciplinarian. I've been in his court a number of times but we never spoke...'

'Ah, dats where he saw you and liked you.'

Tamuno said 'Strict with other people, not with you... I beg... Which time we will come out of this hospital?'

'When the doctor says okay.'

The visitor who called at the house left a card which Titi brought along to the hospital.

Liza examined the gold lettering. 'George Nando! of all people! Father of Obi... Wonder what he wants, and at this time.'

Titi said that he asked about Madam, then insisted on seeing the boy. Titi did not know the connection. He had pressed her to bring out the boy for him to see but she had told him they had both gone for their lesson. He left without seeing Obi.

Liza tried to suppress her fears. She had not heard from him for a very long time. Was he just remembering his son?

Before Titi left she mentioned that the police had called twice asking about her and she told them Madam had travelled.

The constant knocking on the door brought Titi to her feet. She peered through the spy hole and saw two dark figures. The knocking resumed.

Titi ran to the bedroom and woke her Madam.

'Open up! Police!'

Liza heard the voices in the distance. Then Tamuno was at the bedroom door.

'Excuse me... some police are knocking at our door.'

'Let them in.' Hastily she put on a housecoat.

'Are you Barrister Elizabeth Papadopoulous Obi?' said one of them who had tumbled into the room.

'Yes.'

'You're wanted at the Police Station.'

Liza looked beyond the Police Officer who was carrying a Mark Four rifle.

Behind him were two women whom she recognised

as the wives of Saka Jojo. On seeing them she felt her
anger rise but reminded herself to keep calm.

'That's okay,' she said. 'I'll meet you there.'

She drove in her own car, accompanied by
Tamuno.

The Desk Officer asked for a statement.

The wives of Saka had already made theirs.
According to the Desk Sergeant, they claimed that
Liza had attacked them in her own apartment when
they called there to search for their husband.

Liza in her statement, denied knowing them and
claimed that they had laid in ambush for her and
when she came home, they attacked her. Tamuno
corroborated her statement.

The Desk Seargent shook his head: 'Madam, this is
a domestic matter. We Nigerian Police we never like
to interfere in domestic affairs. I advise you, go and
settle this matter. Do you all agree to go home and
keep the peace? If not the matter will be charged to
court. What do you choose?'

'Er? What do you say?'

The wives held a quick consultation. Liza watched
them. There was the buxom but shapely one who
appeared to be the Head wife. They called her Mama
Risi and she carried herself with an air of authority.
The other two, one, called Lady Amina from Zaria
and the other Alero from Warri. They made a dazzling trio, and Liza could see they had money to lavish
on themselves. The consultation lasted two minutes.

Mama Risi said, with decision, 'We go to Court!'

The tall slender one Lady Amina called the others
aside and they began to whisper loud enough for Liza
to hear.

174

'We must teach her a lesson!'

They returned and told the Desk Sergeant. 'We want to go to court!'

'Where is your husband...?' said the Desk Sergeant.

'Or, are you all together?' He pushed his register aside and entered a side room probably to consult someone. He came back.

'We have the same husband,' said Alero.

'You will go upstairs and meet the Prosecuting Officer.'

In the office of the Deputy Commissioner, the three women sat on one side, while Liza and Tamuno sat on the other.

They listened to him for a moment. The wives were adamant. The case must go to court.

'These people are serious,' whispered Tamuno. 'They want to disgrace you. You better deal with them.'

It was all that Liza could do to hold her down. Once she almost slapped Lady Amina had Liza not got up and pulled her back.

The Desk Sergeant began to build up the case file. They remained at the Police Station until the early hours of the morning.

They heard a knock at the door and Tamuno went to open it.

She came back and said, some people from Ogabu.

'Oh! It's about this fighting on the border. Let them come in.'

An old man wearing a wool cap and a felt jumper over a george cloth hobbled into the room. He was accompanied by three women, one dressed in black. They said they came from Ogabu and were sent by Martha Obi, mother of Jagua Nana.

Liza said to them 'Sit down, I am coming.'

They looked about the room and sat down.

Tamuno went to the fridge and produced biscuits and some minerals which she served. They drank in silence.

Liza presently emerged wearing jeans.

She sat opposite them and they told her how they had seen her when she was in Ogabu and had asked where she lived and found her. They had come to her to help them make representations to government for compensation. The woman in black lost her husband to gendamerie fire when he was out by the river, fishing.

Liza took down some more notes and gave them the address of the Old Bailey Chambers in Isale Eko. She asked Tamuno to take them there and wait till she arrived.

She went in and patched up her face before driving there in the Honda. After they had stated their case, the Senior Partner in the Old Bailey Chambers, Barrister Adetona, called Liza into his office and asked what she thought.

'It is a complicated case,' said Liza. 'Whom do we sue?'

'Nobody,' said the S.A.N. 'But we can make a noise. The Federal Government should be made to listen.'

Liza jumped to her feet.

'I've got an idea.'

'What?'

'The television...I can get the Producer to interview them, bring home the story to the government. I heard on the news that the Foreign Minister of Cameroons is arriving in the country tomorrow.'

'That's fine.'

'If the interview is put on...'

'And if the TV team can visit Ogabu and interview many more maybe we can get something.'

'Our Foreign Minister has already asked for compensation for the victims of the attack.'

'What more do we want?'

Liza went back to her office and conveyed the news to the delegation.

They welcomed the idea, but were interested in some concrete move towards their rehabilitation. They begged Liza to find them food and to arrange for their peaceful return to the plantation.

'It's a very complex matter,' Liza told them, 'but we are going to do our best.'

More refugees from Ogabu sat in the sitting room. Tamuno served them with hot soup and cooked yams.

When they had eaten, the old man in the woollen cap talked.

My name be Silas. It's hard for us. We live and work in de Cameroons some in Equatorial Guinea. Dere is no boundary between us and them. Where I live, one side be Nigeria the other side be Cameroon. Dis trouble start long time now...He paused to take snuff and one of the little children began to whimper. The mother stuffed a well filled breast into his mouth and he began to squeeze and suck. She was a young woman in her early twenties with luminous large eyes.

Jagua Nana's daughter leaned forward. 'I cannot understand what you people see there. They fight and kill you and you still keep on going there, what for?'

'What can we do?'

Tamuno and Titi retired to the kitchen while Jagua Nana's daughter took down more notes.

Not today dis palaver start, said the old man. De soldiers from Cameroon use to fight our people. You just siddon in your house, dem rush dere with gun, begin kill everybody. Las time dem kill about twenty soldier from our side. We all pack and run. After when evertin' cool', we go back.

'Meself ah be ol soldier, am an ex-service man. I fight for World War one, ah used to work in PWD Public Works Department after de war, den ah take my pension and go to work for Cameroon. Now evertin' I get done loss.' He paused to fill another nostril with snuff.

Liza pondered over the plight of these people. They had come to her for help. She would not disappoint them. If there was one thing she was now determined to do, it was to help these poor people from Ogabu. Surprisingly the papers in Lagos were not playing it all up the way it should be done. Before the unrest began they had screamed for war. Now that the trouble was in full swing, the news was swept away by other more pressing events.

The old man continued. 'Dem sell me as slave labour after the war! After I demob from army I work in a cocoa plantation. At de time people from

178

different part of Nigeria go dere to work in plantation. Me and about ten people come from Ogabu.

Silas narrated how the recruiting man who sold him used to come to Ogabu in the night and call from door to door painting rosy pictures of fortunes to be made. Silas was one of those lured into going there to seek a fortune. It did not occur to him then that this man was also trying to make money out of them. They did not even care to know that the white men mainly Spanish — were building their own fortunes on their labours. Conditions were bad. The labourers would meet in the night and he, Silas was made leader of demonstration.

One morning, they had all assembled for work. 'We no know say one of us done go report say we can strike.' As they marched in front of the camp commander, he blew his whistle and the soldiers came out and began to fire at random at the workers.

'Only God save my life. I run and hide in de bush nearly two weeks before I reached home. At dat time I never marry. Am young and strong. Not now weh ah done tire and ol'.'

He did not return to Santa Isabel, but changed venue to work in the Cameroons. Things were a little better and he came home once and took back with him this woman who became his wife.

They were living well. She brought her sister to live there and a white man took fancy to her and made her his concubine. She bore two bambinos for him. Then trouble. Now they had run and left all their possessions.

When Liza got to Chambers she found that

the learned counsel Adetona had once travelled
to Bamenda, and knew something about the
situation.

He said. 'Listen. We talk of borders. To the
Western side of Nigeria is Benin Republic. They
speak Yoruba like Nigerians in Oyo. To the
Northeast is Chad, they speak Kanuri, like the
Nigerians in Borno. And to the East you have
Cameroon, they speak English and French. How do
you know a Cameroonian from a Nigerian? Some of
them have lived here for generations. How do you
know a Nigerian from a Cameroonian. Some
Nigerians will not come back home if you offer them
the moon.

'Does that mean we abandon them to die,' Liza
asked.

'Okay, now, lets look at it this way. All we can do is
to write a petition for these people. It's a government
to government affair. High diplomacy.

A knock came at the door. It was Tamuno.

'What's the matter, you look terrified!'

'It's Silas...that old man.'

'Excuse me,' said Liza.

She went to her own chambers.

Tamuno would not sit down.

She said, 'The man is dying...he must be rushed
to hospital at once.'

They rushed downstairs and drove to the house.

Liza had hardly parked the car when Silas' wife
came rushing out a child in each arm. 'Save my
husband.'

They put him all bones and skin, in the car. He
coughed a deep wracking cough.

180

On the way to the hospital he began to cough out blood, then he was silent.

The hospital certified him dead.

'God!' said Liza.

Liza arranged for a Death Certificate, Special Documents to transport the corpse to Ogabu across the country, and funeral expenses.

She was unable to go to Ogabu, but she sent Tamuno to accompany the wife of Silas to her village.

Then she thought: Nigeria is such a tense country. On the one hand Auntie Kate is bringing girls into the country to serve as sex slaves. On the other hand some men are recruiting Nigerians to serve in their countries as slave labour. She could have laughed, but she thought, *How do I come into it?*

She hardly realised it but she was speaking aloud and she was alone. Am I going mental or what?

Tamuno said, 'I see the sign. There will be war!'

Liza could not bring herself to doubt her.

Chapter Ten

The Rivals

A man in a light-blue chauffeur's uniform complete with cap was standing at the door. Parked in the driveway behind him was Saka's Mercedes.

'Masta sent me' said the stranger. 'I am a driver to Saka Jojo.'

He produced a parcel.

From inside the sitting room, Liza said, 'Tamuno, who is it?'

'Master's driver.'

'From where.'

'From Mr. Saka Jojo.'

'I'll be with you in a minute.'

In a moment, Liza was at the door.

'Driver, tell your Master not to send you here again.'

'Yes Madam,' said the driver.

He turned and was leaving when Liza noticed the parcel with Tamuno.

'Return it to him.' Tamuno ran after the driver and returned the parcel.

Since leaving the clinic, Liza had vowed to keep Saka Jojo at a distance until things became clearer to her.

Again the feeling, as she parked the car — dizziness, headache, heart thumping, feet unsteady, mind uneasy.

'If things continue like this, I am going to leave this place — it's getting too hot to stay here.'

'Madam, Madam . . .'

She looked round, startled.

From behind a hedge, she caught a glimpse of Titi beckoning to her.

'What's the matter, Titi?' She noticed that Titi had tied her cloth under her armpits, no scarf or headtie. This meant that she had sneaked out of the house in a hurry.

She continued to beckon. 'Come quick.'

Another ambush? This time she would have to ask for police protection.

She followed Titi.

'Where's Ngozi?'

'I took dem to our neighbour . . .'

'Madam . . . those two men . . .'

'Dat Chief from England who wear bead, and our Masta.'

Liza wanted to tell Titi to stop calling Saka Jojo Master.

'Madam, you better don't enter the house.'

'Why not?'

'Wait till dem fight finish!'

Suddenly the idea of the two men fighting in her sitting room threw Liza into a panic. She raced to her front door and entered the sitting room. Saka Jojo and George Nando were standing eye to eye on the point of exchanging blows.

She planted herself between the two men and pushed them aside.

'What's got into you?'

George Nando, his eyes flashing, said, 'I've told

184

this idiot never to set foot here again. If he repeats it I'll kill him.'

'Who's an idiot?' Saka replied. 'You have no right here. This flat is rented, furnished by me and . . .'

Liza said, 'Oh, dear! Has it come to that, Gentlemen?'

George Nando eyed Saka Jojo and waved his flywhisk in his rival's face. He was slim and tall in an elegant manner and did not appear to Liza like a man who would want to grapple with Saka Jojo who was of medium height and stocky build.

Nando said sarcastically, 'Thank you for putting up the mother of my son. Send me a bill.'

Liza said, 'Gentlemen! I think you better leave. This is scandalous!'

She went into the bedroom, tears in her eyes.

She was the mother of Obi, that was true, but she would not go back to Nando. As for Saka Jojo, after the beating by his wives, the least he could do was leave her alone for sometime. She heard the front door bang, and a moment later George Nando's Rolls started, followed by Saka's BMW.

When the case of the Police versus Elizabeth N. Obi and three others were called up, the police prosecutor was not in court. Liza was represented by Mr. Adetona, one of the counsels from 'Old Bailey Chambers'. The case was adjourned for seven days.

On the seventh day, the wives of Saka Jojo were in court, all dressed in pale blue lace uniform with pale blue headties trimmed with silver, and gold trinkets. The Court was told that the police prosecutor was tied up in another case in another court.

After the third adjournment, counsel for Bebe Jagua argued that since the police were too busy to appear in court, and since the court was too busy for further adjournment, the case should be struck off.

The magistrate bowed his head, exchanged a knowing glance with Liza N. Obi who immediately bowed her head. The judge struck off the case. The lawyers in court murmured as one, 'As the court pleases.'

The wives of Saka Jojo, humiliated, quickly crowded into his waiting Mercedes 280S and drove off amidst whispers in court. The business of the court went on as scheduled, on other matters.

Judge Macros would be working late in his study writing his judgment, thought Liza, as she drove towards his residence. She felt a little uneasy. What was her real motive? Why did she respond to his invitation? Suddenly a car sped past her disturbing her thoughts.

It was a BMW and Saka Jojo was driving. He pulled up on one side of the road and flagged her down. She veered off the road and stopped. Saka Jojo stepped down and came towards her. He wore a white Italian tailored suit, a maroon shirt and white bowtie. His shoes had side buckles which glinted as he walked. His feet made a clacking sound on the pavement.

'Where are you going?'

'My business.'

'You're going to that old judge, not so?'

'Therefore?'

'Turn round and go home now.'

'The cheek of it!' Liza said, 'What's your authority?'

'You're crazy.' And she put her hand down on the steering wheel.

'Let me tell you this, Saka. Your days were numbered — by your wives. No man or woman handles Bebe Jagua that way and gets away with it, you hear me? I'm not a pauper, or a parasite, or a harlot. Just a decent, lonely Nigerian girl trying to make her way in life.' She felt a lump in her throat and suddenly the tears came.

'By sleeping with a judge?' he asked. 'Is that how you will make your way?'

'If you see it that way.' She wiped her tears.

He leaned on the car. Other cars were hooting behind him, but his eyes were like charcoal fire.

'You are wayward and wicked. You think you are liberated. You are still mentally in England. Africa is different. Come home . . .'

'Sorry, I'm not liberated. I just want to be sensible.'

'In love matters, you cannot be sensible. So you've decided it's over?'

She blew the horn, to avoid his seeing the tears which had started filling her eyes again. He stepped back and the Honda Prelude pulled away. Saka Jojo leapt backwards, narrowly missed by the passing traffic. She saw him in the rear-view mirror hands raised in despair.

His anguish made her happy. Perhaps he would learn that money does not buy love.

Judge Okeh Macros smiled at her, hands

extended. The woolly head of greying hair seemed to have been powdered. His skin shone with a youthfulness which belied his fifty-five years. He pulled her towards him and they embraced.

Suddenly she did not feel depressed any more. The words of Tamuno came to her: *the old ones are the best*. In Judge Macros, Bebe Jagua was finding a rare peace.

'At your age, you are still so active?'

'It's you who make me so.'

'Tell me about yourself.'

'There is little to tell. I married the first wife, she developed mental problems. I married the second wife, she chooses to live apart. For years we have tried to patch things up. It has not worked. I'm a disillusioned Judge. There is no justice. I'll tell you this, we are all carpenters in this profession. Our job is to nail the coffin on someone who is dead. We are never present at the killing or at the burial. We just nail the coffin. That is how we must dispense justice.'

'And if you refuse to nail the coffin?'

'You are removed by the powers that be. A servant must be worthy of his hire. We try to be worthy servants.'

'But the judiciary is independent!'

'Who said that? Independent of the opposition, that's the truth. Not of the incumbent.'

'And the law,' said Bebe Jagua. 'If you follow the rule of law in all your judgements...'

There was a pause and then he said, 'You've got it! But you're going to be unpopular with the ruling ones who pay your salary. Follow the rule of law and your court dries up but you will acquire a reputation. Your promotion freezes. No cases will come to your court. Because the law will make it impossible for you to nail the coffin. The dead cannot be buried. And that's embarrassing!'

'Is it as bad as that?'

'It's terrible. High Court litigation takes a minimum of five years. All the witnesses die. Justice flees. The government wrongs a man. The case goes to court. We sit on it. Or — we find a way to dismiss it, or to strike it out. Of course it's not always like that.' He stared at her. 'Am I being bitter? Or just offloading my frustration?'

Then she remembered. This was Judge Macros who had a reputation for judgments defying the government. Few had ever come so near as to hear him bare his soul like this. So this was it! Liza breathed a deep sigh.

'So, I am in the wrong profession?'

'You want to be a judge?' He laughed.

'Some day. But first I have to join the government civil service, start at the bottom . . .'

'Well, I'll tell you this. To every profession there is a dream-side and a reality-side. I am giving you the reality-side of things. You're young, you can keep on dreaming. Nothing stops you from dreaming.'

'Oh yes! If we don't dream the world collapses. If we dream it also collapses but at least we have the consolation of having dreamed. He smiled a pitiful smile. He reached out and touched her. To Bebe Jagua his touch was so comforting.

'When I'm with you I never feel your age,' said Bebe Jagua.

'Age is a matter of the mind. It is like a basket-full

of cassava which you carry on your head,' he said his face brightening.

'It's magic,' Bebe Jagua said. 'My heart is so full, it is bursting.'

Suddenly, Bebe Jagua said, 'Don't send that man to the gallows.'

Judge Macros tensed. 'What man?'

'Any man,' she said, 'Bloodshed is bad. Taking life is worse. Punish them instead. Give them life jail, anything.'

'But what man?'

'I don't know,' she said. 'I'm tired. Let me rest.' She went to the three-seater settee, shut her eyes, and drowsed. She could hear him still worrying as he worked. 'What man, tell me . . . or did you know the judgment I was writing? Oh, Gosh!'

Much later on, she felt a light tap on the shoulder. 'I've finished,' said Judge Macros. 'He did not go to the gallows. He got five years . . . Shall we be going?'

'Thank you, oh, thank you for saving a life.' She kissed him and gave him her hand which he took and squeezed.

When she returned home next morning, she was told by Tamuno that Saka Jojo came in the night looking for her. She took the note he left behind, and read his apology. Then she went to the bathroom and prepared to meet the day.

The BMW drove up to the gate and Saka Jojo, immaculate in his cream safari and snake-skin shoes, stepped out and walked towards the gate.

Titi opened the door. 'Welcome, sah!'

190

'Where's Madam?'

'She travelled.' Liza had given Titi full instructions never to reveal her whereabouts to anyone, not even to Saka Jojo. She wanted time to think. There was the sound of a car door being opened and shut.

Titi looked and saw a chauffeur getting out of a large Mercedes Benz saloon car. The uniformed chauffeur came to the house and asked if Barrister was at home. The judge wanted her to come to the tennis court.

'She travelled,' said Titi.

Saka Jojo, all eyes, asked Titi after the car had driven off, 'That man — he used to come here?'

'Which man?' Titi said, 'I don' know de man sah!'

'You see that car here before?'

'No, sah.'

At that moment, a Rolls Royce pulled up and George Nando came towards the house.

He looked contemptuously at Saka Jojo. 'How often must I tell you not to set foot in this house again?'

Saka said, 'I think this insult has gone on long enough! What the hell!' He crouched suddenly and took a dive at George Nando's legs. Taken unawares, George Nando staggered, was toppled backwards and crashed to the floor. Saka Jojo leapt on him and grabbed for his throat. Nando twisted free, seized a side stool and crashed it into the head of Saka Jojo. Titi and Tamuno raised an alarm, screaming at the top of their voices. Nando's chauffeur ran into the room. He threw himself between the two men and was pummelled on both sides by blows.

The two men began to circle round and round him,

looking for an opening, raining curses all the while. There was a gash on Saka Jojo's head from which the blood was pouring onto his face. George Nando was hatless, his traditional beads, broken and scattered. Both men were panting for breath.

The chauffeur carefully shepherded his master out of the room, upbraiding him for descending so low as to fight. 'Why you don call me to teach am lesson?' He glowered at Saka Jojo and shook a fist at him. 'Don' come near! If you try it, ah jus' kill you for nothin'.' He did not stop warning Saka Jojo until his master was safely in the car.

After they had driven off, Saka Jojo called for a towel and a bowl of water. He cleaned his face and straightened his jacket.

The blood continued to ooze out of the wound until he got into his car and drove off.

'Do you know something,' said Liza.

Tamuno said, 'Tell me.'

'After that attack I've started to wonder...what am I doing here in Nigeria? Must I suffer because I chose to come home?'

'I don't understand. You want to return to England? But does England want you? We need you here in Nigeria. Think of Ogabu people.'

'My father Nick Papadoupolous lived and died in Nigeria. My mother Jagua Nana I now know. My Uncle Brother Fonso does not know me...My step-mother Auntie Kate is on the run, and it's goodbye to Saka Jojo and his wives. So what am I still doing here?'

192

'Are you planning to go back to England?'
Tamuno asked.

'Something like that...In England I can live a
quiet life.'

Tamuno said, 'Nobody will know you there,
nobody will need you. You'll live quiet and die quiet.
But here, in Nigeria, you will live like somebody.
Your mother will be happy and proud, everybody
will love you...'

It struck Liza with sudden force that Tamuno was
speaking the truth.

'Me, I've never been to England, I want to visit
there not to live there. Visit and come back!'

Ngozi and Obi came in from outside and Tamuno
excused herself.

Liza watched her. It pleased her how Tamuno had
been able to win over the children so quickly.
Tamuno had proved a loyal companion and a
confidanté. She had fought Saka Jojo's wives
alongside Bebe Jagua, tended Ngozi and Obi, and
became a vital part of the household.

Tamuno often said, 'I have no children of my
own.'

And Titi had told her, 'Never min, God's time is
best.'

'I need you Liza,' said Saka.

'Not now,' Liza said. 'Give me time.'

She had repeatedly refused to see him, but one act
of carelessness had given him the chance to break into
the room.

She looked into his eyes and was sorry for him. He
was tortured, she could read that. But after the fight

with his wives, things could never be the same
again.

'Listen,' pleaded Saka Jojo, 'I intended to check
into the Federal Palace Hotel, unknown to my wives.
You can come there, and lets talk things over.'

'Not me,' said Liza.

'Liza, it appears you are still angry with me.'

'I told you give me time.' It hurt her to say it, but
there it was.

'I can't believe it,' he said. 'I still think you will
forget everything and forgive. It was not my fault I
was away... I lost millions. As for that old judge...
Forget him.'

Liza smiled. 'The old judge as you call him, is a
nice gentleman and anyway that is not your
business.' She stood up. She tried to hide her
mounting anger but it showed in the flickering eyes.
She walked towards the door and held it open.

Saka Jojo brushed past and she shut the door. She
stood still until she heard the door of his car slam and
the engine start up.

Then she put on her best smile and slipped into an
armchair. Ngozi came and sat beside her.

Tamuno said, 'Let me bring you something to
drink.'

'Not now,' said Bebe Jagua. 'I need to think.'

She must have dozed off. She was hearing her own
voice, hollow and dreamlike.

'Saka, Do you hear what I am saying?... Maybe
you don't know this. I did not grow up in Nigeria. I
see things differently from you. There's just so much I
can take and no more...I was ready to be your
Mistress, to let things remain as they were... but now

194

it's ended. I'm not going to be your fourth wife or take the castaway husband of three women who beat me up — money cannot buy everything... But where were you, anyway? Chasing after your millions!...' She saw his face and it was anguished. She felt no pity for him, only pain.

'Liza! Bebe Jagua, think of old times...'

'I have, and very carefully too, Saka. Leave me alone — it's best this way...'

'And all our dreams?'

'Dreams?... does one not wake up sometime? Ha! Don't be childish.!'

'Mr. I have woken up from the dream. At the time of that dream lets say I was lonesome, a stranger in my country. Didn't know anybody. I needed a guide. I just came back home to Nigeria. I was searching for Jagua Nana...'

'You used me?'

'So did you. It applies both ways.'

Saka was pacing the floor. 'So its come to this!'

'To what?' she challenged him.

'Toughness. Bebe Jagua, tough with me...now...'

'What are you going to do about the pregnancy?' Saka asked.

She was shocked. 'Which one, the one that miscarried?'

'Yes,' he said. Then, 'Pardon — miscarried?' He frowned.

She remembered every detail now.

It was just after they had made love. Bebe Jagua had said to Saka Jojo. 'It has happened again...I know the signs. I'm pregnant.'

Saka Jojo turned in the bed and stared at her, his

eyes unblinking. She avoided his eyes and gazed at
the ceiling as though speaking to herself.

'When I was in my teens a law student Abdul
Stevens knocked me up for the first time. I did not
know anything then. But Ngozi was born. Later I
learnt about contraceptives, but would not use
them ... They were messy and interfered too much.
This was before the pill. Then I got pregnant again.
This time it was another man — a business tycoon
Chief George Nando. I was in love with him. And
Obi was born.'

She sighed. Saka Jojo reached out and played with
her breast. 'You are very fertile,' he said.

'I realised it, and determined not to have anything
to do with men. I kept my word, till you came along.
I cannot resist beautiful elegant men, like you, Saka.'

She had rambled on. Finally, Saka Jojo had said,
'Darling, *congratulations*!'

She turned then and regarded him curiously.
'What do you mean — congrats?'

'I mean, you've given me what I want. I have been
looking for a boy, a son to answer my name.'

'How do you know it's going to be a boy?'

'I feel it this time... If you are planning on
removing it, forget it! I shall provide everything you
need...'

'Like what?'

'Let's start at the beginning... from tomorrow on,
no more going to the office... I shall pay all your
expenses.'

'Kind of you, but not possible! What about the
cases I'm handling?'

196

'Brief another lawyer,' He rose and was walking naked to the fridge.

'Darling, the children! Put something on, you're stark naked.'

He shot back into bed and folded her in his arms. In a moment he was snoring. Liza turned her back on him and uttered a sudden sharp sigh when he grabbed her hips and entered her from the rear. 'God bless me,' he mumbled. 'I am a blessed man.'

A sudden crash startled her and she opened her eyes to find she had been dreaming.

Titi came in from the kitchen to say a plate had slipped and was broken. She showed 'Madam' the fragments.

'Go away,' said Liza. 'Be more careful.'

Those had been happier days, Bebe Jagua thought, and she felt a splitting pain in the head when she realised that Saka Jojo, who had just walked back into the room, had become just another bubble in the illusion called love. The bubble had burst and vanished.

'Do you know what strain I have been under this past fortnight? And there was no sign of you? You were running after your millions . . . If your wives had killed me . . .'

'I lost millions . . . that I can stand . . . Millions can be replaced, but not my Bebe Jagua.' He drew nearer. For a moment she felt that rising urge to yield to his charms. Then she braced herself and he saw the expression on her face and drew back.

Titi came into the room and whispered in her ear.

'If you will excuse me,' said Bebe Jagua and she wiggled out of the room with that magic that stopped hearts beating.

Before she could reach the door, Judge Macros had slid into the room with arms extended. 'Sorry. Am I disturbing anything.'

'No, me lord, come in.'

Liza brightened suddenly. Saka Jojo gave the judge a dirty look as he brushed past them and banged the door shut.

She could faintly hear the BMW start and roar away. She prayed he did not knock down any of the children playing in the courtyard.

'Have you returned?' said Mama Risi.

'What d'you mean?' Saka asked.

'From your lawyer gel frien'. Why don' you bring her to stay with us and suffer with us?'

'Whats your business?'

'Saka, you should know the girl is not for you. You're not lawyer. She will take all your money and still leave you.'

'Money is not everything,' said Saka.

'Shut up!' Mama Risi rose to her feet and tied the cloth more firmly about her waist, a signal for 'seconds out'.

She came near enough to Saka to be eye to eye with him.

'You forget you were nothing...But for me. Mama Risi,' and she struck her breast with the open palm of her right hand. 'But for me, where will you be? Today you want to drive us all away because you see England bottom. Your mouth is watering and

198

you're shaking like a small rat. Lissen! Barrister gel is
not for you, you hear? Go and siddon with your
money.'

Saka Jojo flashed his arm. There was a sharp
whack, and Mama Risi's hand went to the side of her
face. Mama Risi screamed and seized him by the
balls. He yelled. She bent low and butted him full in
the chest. Her weight carried her forward and both of
them crashed against the glass.

Lady Amina charged into the room. Tall and
elegant, she now gritted her teeth with fury. She
pulled Saka by the coat tails as he reared up to seize a
chair. He turned, his mouth agape with surprise. He
dabbed at the blood which was rushing down to his
eyes from a cut in his temple. Mama Risi's children,
two girls, let out a din and the whole place began to
buzz with cries of alarm.

Saka shot his leg backwards and caught Lady
Amina in the groin. She doubled up, eyes popping
out of her head.

'I die,' she cried. 'He has smashed my womb!'

'It was smashed before, you idiot!' shouted Saka,
now thoroughly mad.

'You're a street boy, a gutter boy,' cried Mama
Risi, 'Money miss road, common ruffian. *Jaguda*.'

The main door burst open and a crowd of
neighbours rushed in to separate them. Mama Risi
stood panting, her enormous breasts heaving and
falling like mountains of fire.

Saka Jojo went straight into the bedroom, took his
travelling case and left the house. He drove away in
his Porsche 924 Sports car.

'If only I had not quarrelled with Liza Jagua, this is

the time I should have moved in,' he thought.

He checked in at the Federal Palace Hotel, taking one of the Executive Suites. Every night he went to the Casino and gambled away. He let everything slide and took a good look at his life.

What was it all about? Here he was, a young man who had made it, a man with nearly two million in the bank, a booming bunkering business, shares in a shipping line, in the tobacco industry and in plastics.

He was staying under one roof with his three wives. That was a wrong strategy. He should have separated them. Worst of all, all they ever produced was girls. If he died today there would be no one to answer his name. He was getting on to forty. Even if he had a boy now he would be too old to enjoy his company.

He must do something. He must do something — But what? Abandon them all? Mama Risi had stood by him, built him up. He could not bear to hurt her. If she had any human feeling, she would understand his need for a boy, and marry a girl for him. What was her grouse?

On the tenth day, he was standing before the mirror in an open dressing gown. The door slid open. He thought it was the service. He looked round to see Mama Risi in the room. She was gorgeously dressed in the flimsiest of lace material studded with sequins. Her headtie had been tied aeroplane fashion. Her throat was studded with a gold chain and she had put some gold in her mouth, so that her teeth flashed as she spoke.

'What do you want here?' Saka asked, suddenly apprehensive.

'You're my husband. I've come to stay with you.'

200

He looked at her in her dark glasses which concealed the black eyes from the previous fight. The patch on her forehead was invisible because of the headtie.

'Go away! I want to be left alone. I have come here to work...'

'You know what you came for — not work!'

'Who showed you this place?'

'The same one who showed me the house of your Barrister gel friend showed me this place.' She placed her arms akimbo and cocked a look at him.

'Leave Bebe Jagua out of this.'

'Ah beg-o!' said Mama Risi, and as Saka Jojo watched her she began to undress.

'I told you she does not want you. You will only disgrace yourself. Forget her!'

'Go away!' said Saka Jojo. His voice was weak.

He felt a whipping headache.

She was slow and methodical about it. First she folded her headtie and put it on the dressing table. Then she removed the jewels and set them in an ashtray. Saka stared at her like one mesmerised. The woman was voluptuous, even more so in this hotel room, displaying her well rounded and proportioned dimpled thigh and rich fanny. Who said the slim women were the best? He felt that familiar glow in the loins and shamefully tried to conceal his erection.

'Go away, Mama Risi...Did you not hear me?' But there was no authority in Saka Jojo's voice, and he knew she would ignore him.

'I will go away — afterwards, and leave you to your Egyptian harlots. Or is it not Egyptian harlots you came to look for in the hotel? Or is it Swedish harlots?

Whom are you deceiving? You came to work! hah!'

She came to him and put the long nipple of one breast in his mouth, gagging him.

'Suck Mama Risi bobby, my dear.' She held his head and pressed it down.

He sucked, eyes closed. He felt her arse and became a child. She gave him the second breast, which was smaller than the first. And after a while she slipped into the large bed, pulling him under the sheets.

'The door!' he protested.

'Never min'. This is a Hotel. That's what hotels are for.'

There was a knock at the door.

'Room service!'

'Come in! . . .' said Mama Risi . . . Leave it on the table.'

'Excuse, sah . . . er . . . Ma'

'It's alright, Ma, Sah . . . Oooh! . . .'

The door slid close.

The covers went over Mama Risi.

'You know dat gel you're running after?'

'Which gel?'

'Barrister gel,' said Mama Risi.

'What do you mean?'

'I want you to know . . . Ah hear the gel is Jagua Nana's daughter. You know that? She can never keep to one man. Is good for you to know before you kill yourself. The mother is a born harlot.'

'Don't be funny! I met the mother. She's a nice woman and she has a husband.'

'Who say?'

'I say!'

Saka Jojo turned his back on her. He knew she was

getting her fat but shapely thighs into her flimsy
panties then she was tying her cloth, satiated. By the
time she was fully dressed he was asleep.

He slept like a child.

Chapter Eleven

The Death

'Welcome, Ma,' came the chorus. The girls, breasts swinging, scrambled to take the large Kano leather bag from Auntie Kate. She trusted it only to Afua.

'Anybody ask of me?'

The girl Afua said, 'One woman come here, look for you.'

Auntie Kate said, 'How she be?'

'She tall and fine, she wear English dress, black coat just like lawyer. She said you be her step-mother.'

'It's Liza,' said Auntie Kate, and her manner at once became guarded. 'Bebe Jagua...'

'She say anything?'

'Nothing, only she want to see you.'

'She no lef any message?'

'No, Ma.' There was a puzzled look on Afua's face. The other girls opened her room, and she went in, switched on the air-conditioner and flopped into a deep arm chair. They brought her a roasted chicken, some kenke, dried fish and gari. She stared at the food, not eating.

'Chop now, Madam.'

'Ah no hungry. Take de food away,' Then she spoke what was on her mind. 'Ah wonder who show her de way. Ah wonder why de gel no let me res' Abi ah owe am?'

The girls bustled about the room. Auntie Kate looked at them with some pride. They had all the qualities that attracted men. Youth, fresh complexions, provocative rumps and arrogance, coupled with sophistication. Bringing them into the country had not been easy. Auntie Kate was worried about the escalating bribe she had to keep on paying at the border once the girls over-stayed their visas.

Nigerian employers were not averse to employing them. Nor Nigerian men, to using them to satisfy their lust.

She said, 'Bring the money now.'

Afua brought her some money in a bag. She counted it. 'Only tree hundred naira! Since when do I leave you?'

'Madam, business hard. The men no dey spen' money again.'

As they spoke, a young man hovered at the door. He beckoned to Afua.

Afua went to him. Auntie Kate called the other girl and said, 'You yourself, what you get?'

The girl looked down. She had only one asset. Her skin was fair, almost like that of a Mediterranean girl. I got nothing, Madam.'

'Na so you go dey look like idiot and man will take what he want, he won't give you penny. Abi you done get belly?'

She looked up sharply, 'No, Auntie. Ah never get belly.' She pressed her flat tummy with the tips of her fingers.

'Commot from my face! You good-for-nothing.'

The other girl had dyed her hair in rainbow colours and was fat and jovial. She said to Auntie Kate, 'I dey go club dis night. Some white sailor men done come wit war-ship.'

206

'Bring somethin good,' said Auntie Kate. 'Na money ah want.'

Some of the girls remained in the room, while the others went to their own rooms adjoining. Each room had one double-bed and wardrobe and a dressing table with a full length mirror and fan.

Auntie Kate's room was furnished simply — rug on the floor, deep padded chairs, full length mirror. She preened herself before the mirror and a little of her spirits returned. She still looked prestigious and queenly.

When Alberto Ricardo came, she was still moody and after they had made love, she said to him.

'Remember dat night, de woman who followed me till we drive away — after de lecture?'

'The one you said is your step-daughter.'

'Das right! Dem tell me that she come here.'

Ricardo said, 'What did she want?'

'Ask me, now . . . But who show her de way?'

She brooded, then said, 'What I fear is not de gel, but de mother, Jagua Nana. Dat one fit use axe to cut somebody. What do you advise?'

'Do you fear?'

'Yes, I fear for my life. I don't trust that Jagua Nana.'

'But what have you done? Why should they want to harm you?'

'We live togedder at Jos,' said Auntie Kate, then paused.

'Is a long story,' she said. She sat before the mirror brushing her hair. It was real hair and rich. She wore it long. She said. 'Dat Jagua Nana woman you see, dat time ah get one lover white Tin Miner who want me to born pickin for him. Ah no fit conceive. I arrange make Jagua Nana meet de man. By grace of God, Jagua Nana conceive and born a gel chil.'

'Den I take de child, and tell my man dat na me born Liza, and I tell de mother of Liza dat de pickin die for riot.'

Ricardo whistled. 'A serious crime indeed! Abduction, forgery, impersonation, false prentences . . .'

Auntie Kate went on. 'But I tink everything is now over. Is a long time now, over twenty years. De man Nick Papadopoulous die. De girl Liza done grow up and is a free woman. I don't worry her. What more remain?'

'You sure there's nothing else?' Ricardo said.

'Oh yes de will . . . Papadopoulous leave all his money to me before he die, but Liza get some share. I never tell her anything about dat.'

Alberto Ricardo shook his head.

'This sure is complicated.'

He thought for a while.

'You should report to the police, but what are you going to tell them, what are you going to say . . .? If Jagua Nana decides to seek legal redress . . .'

'I don't trust those people,' said Auntie Kate.

'We can go to the police for advice, and protection.'

The Police Commissioner said, 'Madam, what can I do for you?'

Auntie Kate coughed slightly and sat on the bare wooden bench.

'I need police protection,' she said. 'You people no dey get good chair for police station?'

208

'This is a police station Madam not a luxury hotel.'

The Commissioner looked up from his papers. Before him sat this middle-aged woman of outstanding beauty and composure with a velvet-skin complexion, luminous eyes and pouting lips. Beside her sat a man who was definitely not Nigerian. Alberto Ricardo did not say a word.

The Police Commissioner picked up the phone and dialled. 'Is that Crime Department? Send Alabi here.'

As he spoke an officer came in. 'Alabi listen to this lady. Say it again, Madam.'

'I said I need police protection... Somebody is about to kill me.'

'But why? How do you know that?'

'Is someting dat happened a long time ago... now de person is looking for me.'

'The person?'

'The woman. I stole her daughter... but the daughter is grown up and is a free woman for herself. I don't see why dey are worrying... maybe is because of de money...'

'What money?'

'De fadder of de girl leave some money before he die, and I was his wife, so I'm entitled...'

'Wait, wait, wait... not so fast. You will have to follow this officer and make a statement. We will have something on file, then we will decide for ourselves whether you need police protection or not.

'Where do you live?'

'Ikeja.'

'What is your business?'

'Am a Trader.'

'In what line.'

'All lines, anyone for profit, dat's all . . . so when I travel, I bring in new market everytime.'

'You cross the Border?'

'Is de only way you can bring new market and get new customers.'

'So when you travel, you go out of town; and when you find your goods, you come and sell. Is that so?'

She smiled. 'Just so.'

'Go with this officer now and put it all down in writing.'

'Thank you very much.'

The officer led the way. Auntie Kate followed and Alberto holding her by the waist helped her through the door. They climbed one flight of stairs and the officer preceded them into a bare room with more wooden benches, one window and no fan. The air in the room could cook a goat.

'That's how we work here,' the officer said, sensing their discomfort. 'Siddown there.' He pointed to a wooden bench, made shiny by years and years of bottoms rubbing against seasoned wood. From his file he took out a piece of paper and handed it over to Auntie Kate. 'Write your statement here.'

The girls trooped in and out of the bathroom. Sometimes three or four of them remained there. They were undergoing all kinds of beauty treatment. Some were busy wringing the rainbow-coloured dyes out of their hair, others smeared their faces with cream. All of them were bare-footed, with the flimsiest cloth tied under the armpits.

In an adjoining room, Auntie Kate sat before a

large mirror while the girls worked her over, massaging, applying cream while waiting for her hair to dry. The air smelt of burning human hair mixed with evaporating chemicals and cigarette smoke.

Auntie Kate said, 'Wey de policeman?'

'He dey for outside.'

Afua went towards the door, wriggling her bottom, and peeped.

'Ah no see am.'

A hurried search was made and the policeman was found under a tree buying fruits while a girl, Ajua leaned on his shoulder. Ever since he was posted to guard Auntie Kate, he had developed a special liking for Ajua.

A car drew up outside. It was Alberto Ricardo. He came into the salon and sat among the girls. His eyes were averted as one girl passed in front of him, swinging her round ass provocatively. In the presence of Auntie Kate, the policeman was an innocent onlooker.

Auntie Kate stood up, turned this way and that, and strolled towards the bedroom.

'What's he doing outside?' asked Ricardo.

'Who?'

'You know who I mean — the police.'

'Bodyguard.'

In the room, Auntie Kate narrated her fears. She told Alberto that she was uneasy. She had heard that young Liza who was now a Barrister woman was after her with the mother. Worse still, she was told that Jagua Nana was making inquiries everywhere, even at Jos.

'You are exaggerating,' said Alberto. 'Get rid of

him. I told you not to accept him. You went back on your promise! Get that cop out of here. He can't save your life!'

'You wan dem to kill me?'

'Get rid of him.'

Alberto stormed out of the room.

Auntie Kate considered the order. Alberto was influential in getting her what she wanted. If he said get rid of the policeman, she would. Still she hesitated.

A girl came into the room and told her that she was wanted outside. She excused herself and followed the girl into their own room. A man in gold bangles, rings on every finger, said 'I bring de material.' His entire face was covered in a glossy black beard.

He threw down on the table, a bundle of contraband. Money was exchanged. The man left. Then he came back and said, 'Ah no go come again. Customs nearly catch me. I take bush way cross de border . . . Madam, what about de odder money now?'

'Ah still owe you?'

'Nearly twenty thousand,' He smiled an oily smile and rubbed his thick hands together.

'Ah never collect all de money.'

Suddenly the man leered at her and poked her in the ribs with steely fingers. 'You better hurry. How about dis one?' From his hip pocket he produced a small bundle. She opened it and found a white powdery substance. 'What is this?'

The man laughed. He could go from laughter to anger in a flash. He put it back in his pocket. It was after he had left that she was told by Afua that she could make a lot of money selling that powder. It was bought by rich men. When sniffed it had the power to make a person high and utterly callous.

In the night the same man stumbled into the room. He was wounded. She sheltered him and took him to a herbalist. A bullet was removed from his right thigh. They kept him under cover for some time.

When the policeman who was on guard duty asked questions, they gave him a room with Afua. He put his gun aside for the night that Afua spent with him.

During that week, Afua woke up one morning and asked about Auntie Kate. Auntie Kate had not returned, and this was unusual, for Afua knew she had not left the country.

At one o'clock, she grew restless. She went into Auntie Kate's room. A touch on the door and it fell backwards. Someone had been there, and the room was in a shambles. There, on the floor, with a dagger through her left breast lay Auntie Kate. She must have been dead for some time.

When the police arrived to investigate there was no one who could tell them what had happened. The policeman on duty lay in a stupor in Afua's room. He was wearing only a light kente cloth, loaned to him by Afua. His uniform was draped over his Mark IV rifle, but he was still breathing lightly. He could not say by whom, but he knew he had been drugged. His eyes were glazed and he looked stupid when asked what had happened.

From the Cameroons came the news that Nigerian troops and Cameroon troops were exchanging shell fire. The villagers on both sides of the border were all packing their belongings and fleeing to safety.

A chill wind swept through the girls' hiding places. 'What is going to happen to us?' Afua asked. 'Auntie Kate brought us here. Now, she is dead, and not only that, there is war on the border.. We are lost! Oh, God!'

Liza made her way to the Cameroons Embassy. The entrance was barricaded with suitcases, baskets of personal belongings, pots and pans. The Charges Des Affaires recognised her and was waving frantically at her.

'Come and help me talk to these people! I tell them the luxury bus is coming to take them all home. It will stop at Mamfe via Calabar. From there they will find their way home to Bamenda or Beaua.

Liza overhead some remark, 'We're just like refugees . . . only no *kwashiokhor* . . .'

'Attention! Attention! The bus is here . . . move on to Onikan Park. It is waiting for you. Your loads will go in a separate trailer . . . the bus is for passengers only. Leave your baggage behind . . .

Pandemonium broke loose. Those to pity were the women with four, five children. The link with Cameroon had been long and good. Liza felt that this could not be the end.

'Taxi!' Liza waved but the yellow Peugeot with the green stripes sped away without stopping. The taxi veered off the road and crashed into a *molue* bus laden with hanging monkeys.

The taxi driver and the *molue* driver came out of their vehicles and people began to yell as though Mighty Igor was trying to floor Mill Mascaras.

The heat was unbearable.

214

What they were saying everywhere as the big buildings burned and the Heads of States talks went on, was that Cameroons had pushed Nigeria to the wall. This was not time for lectures on border clashes. It was time to go to war.

News came of a big manouvre somewhere. Nigerian planes, Nigerian tanks, Nigerian infantry, rolling along the highways to the borders.

But no war had been declared — yet. People were waiting for war to be declared. The Foreign Ministers of the border countries were recalled by their governments from the campaigns overseas against Nigeria. All was tense.

Everyday the radio talked about 'Territorial Integrity, 'Sovereign State'. The refugees were taken by sea back to their homes. Some crossed over by land. Nigerians were returning to Nigeria from other countries. Non-Nigerians were moving from Nigeria into their own border countries. On the border brisk immigration business was going on. The items of trade were passports, visas, identity cards.

And suddenly it was all over. The Heads of State of Cameroon, Niger, Chad, Benin Republic jointly on television announced that they had reached an accord.

Judge Macros said to Liza, 'Will it last?'

'I don't know,' said Liza. 'I wish it would.'

He said. 'I have put in my papers for retirement.'

'You did well, love.'

'I am taking the initiative.' He pulled her close and patted her tight fanny. His eyes were twinkling. Whenever he patted the shapely rear of Jagua Nana's daughter, his eyes always twinkled.

'You are my sugar daddy,' she cooed.

'And you are my sweet sixteen, and you give **me** life.'

She disengaged from him and wiggled across the room in a pair of silk slacks that responded to every inflexion of her movement. The silk blouse was unbuttoned.

'Jagua Nana's daughter, you are going to kill me.'

'You just said I give you life. How can I kill you?'

'I'm confused. What are we going to do?'

'Just go on loving.'

'And living?'

'Yes. My mother Jagua Nana approves.'

'Talking about living. We have two places to go to — Ogabu, to see your grandmother and the Lagos-Benin Expressway to see Jagua Nana and Tobias Momoh — lovely couple.'

Liza said, 'Have you not forgotten something?'

'What?'

'Badagry. Your home town.'

'Oh yes! You want to go and see the relics of the Macros family . . . I forgot, but it's just an hour or two by road from here. When they talk about border-clashes and wars and so on, I just laugh. We live on the border and the Benin people are our brothers.' He paused and a smile lit up his face. 'We speak the same language. When you get to the border — there is no border.

'We are all African brothers and sisters. It's the whites who are dividing us. I hope the Heads of States are not stupid enough to fall to Western propaganda.' He said, 'Come near.' And she came and he held her and pulled her close.

'Sit on my lap.'
'You can't carry my weight. Sugar Daddy.'
'Try me. love bird.'

Chapter Twelve

The Mortuary

The Mortuary Attendant had a face like death itself, with pale watery eyes, rough upper lip and chin, a wet mouth from which he kept wiping off the saliva with the sleeve of his *danshiki*. The *danshiki* may have been white, but that must have been years ago, before he recovered it from some destitute corpse. Bebe Jagua recoiled when he got close enough to allow her a smell.

'A tall woman!' he repeated.

'Like queen,' said Jagua Nana. 'Not long since dem bring am here.'

The attendant's eyes seemed to glow all of a sudden.

Liza was trying to make out whether the man was drunk, insane, or both, or whether working among the dead had twisted him into some freak zombie clown.

After a while, Liza and her mother stopped talking. The silence echoed. They stared at each other, with fear in their eyes.

The man came out of his stupor and said 'The lady . . . she is in here . . . Yes. She came in three days ago. Follow me.'

He spoke of the dead woman with the same courtesy one would extend to the living. Liza and her mother hesitated. The man had raced swiftly down the cemented slope of the mortuary basement and had turned a corner. Something about his feather-light movement reminded Liza of a ghost. She took the first hesitant steps and dragged her mother along.

'Are you afraid?', the man leered, re-appearing... 'Nothing to fear. I stay with them everyday.'

'You stay with dead people...?'

He opened a door and a gust of chilly wind smoked towards Liza and Jagua Nana.

They found themselves in a large hall, with a kind of shelving system. Small chrome handles glinted everywhere, for opening each cupboard. From each one, a label dangled.

The grey-bearded attendant on his toes, pulled at one of the handles, and expertly slid out the contents which lay on a stretcher.

It was a woman, beautiful even in death, with a placid expression. It was Auntie Kate, on closer examination. The mortuary attendant pointed at the wound beneath the left breast. 'See where dem chuk am.'

Jagua and Liza gasped.

'So this is the end!' Liza looked away.

Jagua tip-toed nearer, arms folded.

She said, 'Auntie Kate! Answer me! Na so we meet? Kate, you no wait make you tell me why you tief my pickin?'

'Mama she's not hearing you.' Liza pulled at her mother's dress. But Jagua Nana did not heed her daughter. The mortuary attendant stood quite still, humming a tune.

Auntie Kate was lying on her back, with her hands crossed in front of her sex. From where she stood, Liza could see other corpses inside the large dimly-lit

220

chamber. The windows of air were all inter-connected, as in an open fridge, so that the cold air circulated to each and every dead body. Here was no distinction, Bebe Jagua reflected. They all lay silent, bathing in the last luxury of the cold air before their next-of-kin or close friends came to claim them for mother earth's consumption.

'Let's go, mother,' Bebe Jagua was shivering. 'I feel afraid.'

The dizziness and nausea were coming.

'Dem take knife kill am,' said the mortuary attendant. He moved smartly, pulling Liza to the other side of the body. Liza recoiled from his stiff and chilling grip. She allowed herself one brave look and saw the stab wound.

'I am supposed to know something about her death,' Liza mumbled to herself.

Just then a policeman carrying a rifle came out of a corner. He wanted to yell at them, but when he saw Jagua Nana on her knees, deep in prayer and Bebe Jagua praying beside her, he himself had no option but to remove his cap, kneel down and make the sign of the cross.

May de souls of de faithful departed, trough de Mercy of God, rest in peace, Jagua Nana intoned.

'Amen,' said Bebe Jagua.

They rose. In silence, they walked along the cemented slope. Their steps made a ghostly echo. At last they emerged in the sunshine. As they were leaving the mortuary they saw Alberto Ricardo arrive, accompanied by more police. Behind them was a hearse used by the Town Council for burials. Alberto had probably come to claim the body for burial in the public cemetery.

Why? They were good friends.

Bebe Jagua preferred not to speak to him. If Alberto recognised her, he did not show any sign. To her mother Liza said, 'So Alberto Ricardo is the one to bury Auntie Kate?'

'Na dem palaver,' said Jagua Nana.

Tobias was waiting for Jagua Nana in the Range Rover. Liza entered her Honda. She sat for some moment collecting herself before driving homewards. From the rear-view mirror she saw the policeman beating the mortuary attendant with the butt of his rifle.

Before entering the house, Bebe Jagua called for a bucket of water and washed her hands, face and feet. Then she entered and sat down, not eating, not drinking, just thinking about life and death and still not convinced that Auntie Kate was dead and gone.

'Are you Elizabeth Nene Papadopoulos?'

'Yes.'

The policeman, carrying a Mark 4 rifle made no effort to come in.

Liza stood barring the door, with Tamuno and Titi standing close beside her.

'You're wanted at the Police Station.'

'What for, this time?'

'There's a report against you.'

'May I know the nature of the report?'

'Till we get there.'

Panic seized her. She thought: whom can I contact now? She thought of the 'Old Bailey Chambers,' of Judge Macros, of Saka Jojo. The latter was out of the question now. She no longer looked to him for any kind of support.

The constable appeared to be a man of few words. He turned to his companion who was also carrying a Mark 4 Rifle.

Jagua Nana's daughter said, 'Let me put something on.'

They bundled her and Tamuno into the car and drove to the Police Station. Tamuno sat beside Jagua Nana's daughter, while Titi, at first wanted to follow them but was told to remain behind and take care of Ngozi and Obi.

At the Police Station, Jagua Nana's daughter was shown to the office of the commissioner.

The commissioner said, 'About some weeks ago, a woman came here. Her name: Kate Nene Papadopoulous. You know her?'

'I do.'

'She reported she was being traced by yourself, and a certain woman called Jagua Nana.'

'My mother.'

'So you know about it?'

'Go on.'

'She was afraid for her life. She asked for police protection.'

'What!'

'We gave her the protection.'

'How do I come into it?'

'Well, like this. Auntie Kate is dead. She was stabbed to death at her home in Ikeja.'

'Wait a minute, I know Auntie Kate is dead?' Liza must not show them it was no longer news to her.

The commissioner nodded.

'And you think I have something to do with her death?'

'Not directly. We have to go by the report.'

Jagua Nana's daughter felt a cold shiver.

'You will make a statement,' said the commissioner.

She was taken to the next room to make a statement.

'I am afraid I have to keep you in custody until I am satisfied you can be released.'

It was at this point that Jagua Nana's daughter decided to send a quick message to the 'Old Bailey Chambers'! Barrister Adetona could not be found till well into the morning.

He provided bail in the sum of two thousand Naira and Liza was allowed to drive home but had to report to the Police Station every morning at nine.

As police investigations intensified, the news filtered out that Auntie Kate was a border-trade woman who used her wide contacts on both sides of the border to her own advantage. She had been visited by this stocky, heavily-bearded middle-man, and an argument arose for a refund of sums of money advanced to get the girls into Nigeria from across the border. It was speculated that he must have stabbed her to death and fled.

Liza was reading a daily newspaper. It was one of those that had whipped up interest in what they called THE SEX-SLAVE MURDER.

They had managed to find and publish a picture of Auntie Kate whom they described as 'The brain behind a smuggling syndicate, a woman who was a

224

sex-slave dealer in young girls imported from across the border.'

The paper said her murder occurred under 'mysterious circumstances' and though no arrests had been made Nene Papadopoulous, was expected to help the police with investigations.

The first day the case was called, the court-room and court premises were packed full.

'Court! . . .'

The Court rose and bowed.

The magistrate, a woman in her fifties, returned the bow and sat down. She frowned and began to write in a large register.

Rustling in court. Lawyers turning pages of their tomes. A lady stood up and called out:

'Case No. LG/42/73N.'

'The State versus Liza Nene Papadopoulous and three others.'

Jagua Nana's daughter saw Afua, one of the girls who had received her the day she went to Ikeja. Afua standing in the dock looked as if she had not slept, or had been beaten up in the cell by the other prisoners, even ravaged. She was guarded by three female police.

'Defendants present in court,' said the lady Registrar.

The Magistrate wrote on.

A lawyer from 'old bailey chambers' rose. 'Your worship, I stand for the Defendant.'

A man rose in all dignity and said, 'I stand for the Prosecution your worship.'

'May it please your worship, we are unable to find the case file, and besides, police have not completed their investigations.

Commotion ensued. The case was adjourned for six months. Liza was bailed and Afua waved to her in a lonely appeal, as she was whisked away into the Black Maria.

Before three months were over, a man described by the newspapers as a wanted smuggler, was arrested and formally charged with the murder of Kate Nene Papadopoulous, over a minor argument about a debt of twenty thousand Naira.

On the day of the final adjournment, the accused stepped down from a Black Maria. There was some confusion and a scuffle, the accused man started running. Two rifle-burst cracked.

He fell and began to cough blood. Before they could get him to the hospital, he was dead.

Chapter Thirteen

The Kidnap

When she got back from taking the children to school, Titi said to Liza, 'Madam, I see that man who come here las' time. The one who fight with masta. He come for school.'

'Which man?'

'That man. Tall, who dress like Chief, he wear red cap and beads.'

'Oh!' She smiled. 'George Nando. What about him?'

Liza was seated before the dressing mirror with Tamuno standing, comb in hand, parting and brushing her hair. She often helped her with zips and buttons and ironed her dress in the mornings. Tamuno also continued to teach Liza to wear accra dress and lace and george and to feel truly Nigerian.

Titi watched Tamuno at work on her Madam, then continued.

'He go into the headmistress office. After the children enter class, I leave him there.'

Tamuno paused, lifted the accra dress she was ironing, and said, 'I don't trust that man. I'm sure he has gone to school for some bad thing... perhaps to see Obi.'

'Is that bad?'

'You know what he will tell the boy? After all, he's the father.'

'But where was he all this time?'

'Will Obi ask him that? You know small boys **and** Daddy!'

'He can see the boy,' said Liza, but she felt weak at the knees.

She stopped suddenly.

She noticed a grin on Tamuno's face.

And then it struck Liza. George Nando in the school. He had been here a few weeks ago and had demanded his son. She had denied him. He had virtually asked her to marry him and return with him to England. She had refused.

'This place is too complicated for you,' he had said.

'Nigeria? One's home — complicated?'

'Yes. You are *naïve*, you cannot tolerate the intrigue, the double-crossings, the treatchery... Come with me to England. I'll give you everything. You'll practice your law and bring up your son to be a decent citizen...'

She beamed. 'Of England?' By the way, are you proposing marriage?'

'Why not. I want you. I've always wanted you as my wife. You know that. Instead you return here, get entangled with that irresponsible idiot, Saka, and now the doting old Judge.'

She laughed outright. But she was tempted.

'Give it all up,' he said. 'Come back with me to the U.K. — not as a student this time, but as the wife of a rich Nigerian — George Nando the shipping magnate.'

Liza hung on to his words. Then she heard her mother's voice... saw the magnificence of Jagua Nana and her man Tobias Moma, thought of grandma Martha Obi, of the refugees from Ogabu who had lost everything in the border clashes and needed her. In England no one would *need* her in the same way.

She shook her head.

'You mean you're not coming?' His eyes were getting redder and redder. He may have been drinking, she thought.

He burst out, 'Then what about the boy? I want to take my son away! He's mine, you know!'

She flared up. 'You want to take him to some *mean* stepmother?' She was screaming. 'No! I suffered enough from stepmothers. No, no, no — George Nando. Obi needs me now more than ever. He's growing. I can take care of him and love him more than any stepmother...'

The pain began to throb in her temples. She raised her hand and touched her brow. She felt suddenly weak.

To her surprise, George Nando, said 'As you say.' The change in his face was sudden. She felt relieved and rose.

And now, Tamuno was smiling with some secret knowledge.

'Madam,' Tamuno said. 'That man loves his son Obi *too much*.'

'So?'

'I think you better find out what he went to the school to do.'

Panic.

A thousand thoughts rushed into Liza's mind. No. It was unthinkable. Kidnapping was left to low people, not Chiefs like George Nando.

But some parents do it. They quarrel over their

kids, and it is from the schools that they kidnap back their children and hide them away.

No, no, no.

'Hurry up, Tamuno.'

She was dressed in less than she imagined.

The children would either be in assembly now, or would be on their morning parade. It would be easy to check.

God! Was it going to happen to her *twice* in her lifetime? As a child she had been stolen, kidnapped, reported dead to her mother. Auntie Kate's selfishness had disrupted her entire life, though she could not say now whether it would have been better or worse, but it would have been *different*. And now George Nando, powerful businessman. What were his plans?

Tamuno and Titi, got into the car. They drove impatiently through the 'go-slow' and arrived at the school. Two security dogs were mounted at the gate but the handlers let them in.

Liza felt reassured.

She was not allowed to see the principal until the children came back from parade and entered their classes.

She caught a glimpse of Ngozi who ran towards her and said, 'Mummy, did you come for Obi too?'

'Who else came for him?'

'His father.'

'And where are they.'

The principal arrived.

'What's going on?'

'This is my mother,' said Ngozi.

'How do you do?' They shook hands.

'I've just come to give a message to my son.'
'What's his name?'
'Obi. He's in class two.'
'Everybody seems to want Obi this morning. Go to the waiting room. You'll find him with his father.'

In the waiting room, there was no Obi, no father, nobody.

At the gate they were told that a man answering the description of George Nando had passed that way, followed by a boy.

By this time Liza was certain that George Nando had lured Obi away. She thought fast. He would not remain in Nigeria. He must have prepared and kidnapped him intending to fly out to England. She immediately went to the commissioner of police and made a report. She begged that a telegram be sent to Interpol that George Nando be intercepted with the boy.

Checking the flights she learnt that a plane bound for Britain had departed that morning at ten, to arrive in London between three and four p.m. with stop one in Libreville before reaching London Heathrow.

'Tamuno what should I do?'
'You have done everything.' Just be patient.
'Should I go to England?'
'Not yet.'
'How can I continue without my son?'
'God dey. You will soon get your son back.'
'I am the mother of Obi. I don't want a stepmother for him, like Auntie Kate was stepmother to me.'
'We will wait for results,' said Tamuno.

She could not do more. She had contacted the

Airline and got them to send a radio message to London.

Looking through the manifest she had seen the name George Nando, and further down the list Obi Nando. It was clear now. They were on the plane. It was simply a matter of time.

Jagua and her daughter entered the bedroom leaving Tobias and Tamuno in the sitting room watching the TV. Ngozi sat at a table, reading. Since the disappearance of her brother, she had become heavy with grief. She moved over and sat near Tamuno.

Jagua Nana looked deep into Liza's eyes. Liza said, 'Mother — what am I to do?'

'You jus' be patient. Dis matter delicate. De man want you and he want de pickin'.'

'Should I go to England?'

Jagua said, 'If you go, you no go come back.'

'I want to stay in Nigeria . . . I don't want to live in England. They need me here. They don't need me in England.

Jagua said, gazing at her daughter with loving eyes, 'Since I see you, my heart done cool down. No more *jaga-jaga*, no more *kata-kata*. Ah done grow up . . . If I die now, I mus' surely reach heaven. If to say I know you dey alive for some place, I for come fin' you where you dey and I for become annoder woman, not de Jagua Nana way everybody know, my life for different. For dis reason ah curse Auntie Kate. De wicked woman. God no go forgive am.'

Liza said, 'She has no conscience. But her Maker will judge that one.'

'She make me to have no respect. Everybody tink

say ah have no pickin of mah own.'

'You have respect. You are my mother, that's all. Ah — ah! Why do you worry?'

Something in Liza's voice touched off the tears and they came streaming down Jagua Nana's face. Liza noticed that her mother's nose was running. She took out a clean handkerchief and wiped her nose for her.

'You're my daughter Bebe Jagua, true to God. Na jus now ah see de resemblance. But you resemble your fadder more. Your nose jus like him nose. Nick is a very fine man, and kind.' Jagua straightened her face. She said, 'You be my daughter, so I must tell you everything. 'Am just a woman who no get anybody. When ah leave my husband, ah don't stay permanent wit any man. Dem call me Jagwa, because ah dress by fashion, and men like me, am social. And ah follow man, if de man is fine and he get money, why not? So till I meet one teacher. Dem call de man Freddie, Freddie Namme. De man no get money but ah like am and I take all my savings money sen' am to England to study lawyer, like yourself.

'You know what de Freddie man do? He take my money marry young girl wit standing breast, and dem stay for England, born two picken. When he return with Nancy and two small pickin, instead of him to stay quiet, he join politics, dem kill am. Ah cry till ah nearly die.'

'Ah visit dem country, Krinamah. Na dere de Chief Ofubara he like me too much and say he go marry me, after when ah settle de quarrel between him people from Krinameh and him brodder people for Bagana. Na big ting — O!'

'You know somethin?' As you dey for Englan' I no

know say you dey dere ah tink dat ah never born pickin.' One day God bless me and give me one son. Ah call de boy *Nnochi*, meaning *de one God take replace de man who die. But de boy no* live long.

'Let me tell you, my daughter. I suffer too much. If I tell you say ah no suffer, na lie. Ah get one friend, Rosa. We dey together for Gunle. Den Rosa marry. De day when ah go to dem house, de young man David entertain me well. Den ah see Rosa Pickin' ah cry. Ah beg God, I say why you treat your Jagua Nana bad, you no even give am one pickin' to hol.'

'When de news reach me say ah get one daughter, ah nearly crase. Dem tell me say na dat woman Auntie Kate tief mah pickin go fin' favour for Nick. Ah tell God, let me take my eye see de woman. Ah go kill am.

'From Krinameh ah begin look for am. Den God take me go Akwanga. Na dere ah meet dis man Tobias. Like say we know ourself before. De man like me one time.

'After dat, life change for me — O! Ah no go tell you lie. Till de day me and you we meet for rest house. Dat day, oh God bless me! Ah take my eye see my own pickin, a big woman, wey fin pass everybody. What ting ah want again for dis worl'? Is finish. If I die now...'

Liza let her unburden herself. She talked about sin, about suffering, about forgiveness. Who was she not to forgive Auntie Kate, especially now that she was dead? God created her infertile, but instead of acepting, she chose to steal another woman's child so as to retain a man's love. The tears were running again. She hugged Liza and both of them cried, then dried their tears. Now Bebe was wiping a running nose. They dried up their faces before returning to the sitting room.

George Nando swore — never again — if he ever got to London in one piece, that it would never happen again. It was the worst, the most troublesome, meddlesome flight he had ever undertaken.

At the check-in counter, he lost Obi and had to search for him for twenty minutes. Eventually he found him just about to board a taxi and slapped some sense into him.

The boy refused to take the sweets offered. Sweets, for goodness sake. How did he suspect they were drugged? Still George Nando was not a man you could deny for long. He had a small syringe in his suitcase and as soon as the boy showed any signs of becoming restless, he would jab him.

One of his friends caused him embarrassment. He was a businessman on the regular route and, noticing George Nando with Obi standing beside him, came near and engaged him in conversation for nearly ten minutes.

Who was the boy? Hello, son? You travelling. Starting school, Chief, never knew you had a son ... What a nuisance. Nigerians were so neighbourly.

At last they got on the plane. The flight was bumpy to start with. Yes it was a DC 10, with a good record on the West African route. No accidents. Yes, no accidents.

He must go to the gents.

He left.

When he returned he found Obi talking in deep

earnest with the Flight Stewardess.

'What was he telling her?'

He sat down beside them and the stewardess left.

She came back with some hot tea and snacks. She stood around. She was an attractive girl, new on the route. If his mind were less occupied — no, he would not trust her now.

The pilot announced that they were crossing the Mediterranean.

Somewhere along the journey, one of the crew came out of the cabin, a young man, not smiling. He tapped George Nando on the shoulder of his *agbada*.

'You George Nando?'

He said, 'Yes, and so?'

'Just wanted to know.'

He left, and went to the back of the flight deck, again talking with the flight stewardess.

George Nando tried to suppress his alarm, now growing into panic. The boy leapt to his feet shouting.

The crew crowded round him.

'It is nothing,' said George Nando. 'He's only dreaming. He gets these fits.'

'Anything we can do to help?'

'No.'

'You taking him to hospital?'

'Something like that.'

All was calm. It was about eleven in the morning. The plane would be in London at three p.m.

There was a white woman on the flight who kept looking at him. He was used to being given the come-on look by women, but each time he tried to respond, she buried her face in a fat novel she was reading. He

236

learnt later on that she was the security officer on the flight.

When they got to Heathrow Airport, he lost her. All appeared peaceful and quiet. He stepped down from the plane, and the boy again embarrassed him by lying down. He refused to walk. George Nando tried to carry him and failed. He was too heavy. He tried again. The boy resisted.

What happened after that was a kaleidoscope.

Identity cards flashed in his face. He was taken aside into a small room. He was questioned by London Customs Officers and kept there. The boy Obi was taken to hospital for examination. The report came back that Obi was suffering the effects of sedation.

Police arrived. George Nando was bundled into a London Police Rover 2600 Saloon with flashing blue lights on the roof.

Meanwhile a message had arrived at the Nigerian High Commission, that Commissioner should intercept Geroge Nando's flight and detain a boy called Obi Nando who had been kidnapped from school by his father and was being forcibly taken to live in London against his mother's wish. Report had been made at the highest level in Nigeria and in London by the mother of the boy, a legal practitioner, saying Mr George Nando had no right to take him away as he was under age.

The High Commissioner on arriving at Heathrow Airport was told that all the passengers had dispersed. Some time later he was able to trace Obi Nando to St. George's Hospital where he was under treatment. When the hospital was completely

satisfied that the boy had recovered, the evidence was
handed over to police who instituted action at the
Old Bailey.

Liza heard about it in Lagos and flew to London.
She stated in court that she did not want George
Nando prosecuted. All she wanted was for her son to
be returned to her. It was a family matter.

The ritual of releasing George Nando took another
month involving several side issues like the validity of
his visa and his business activities, but in the end he
was set free and Obi flew back with his mother and
George Nando resumed his business flights.

Liza told him, 'You can have your son back —
when he grows up. But for now, he remains with me.
Come and see him any time you want to.' She tapped
Obi on the back of the head, 'Son, let's go. Your father
will be in Nigeria soon.' Obi nodded. Together they
went downstairs to the waiting London Taxi and
headed for Heathrow Airport.

Through the window they waved at Chief George
Nando and a very attractive woman who was
standing beside him scowling.

'Who is that?' Obi asked.

'His London wife,' said Liza. 'She has no child of
her own and wants to be your stepmother.'

'I don't like her.'

'Nor do I,' said Liza.

London was wrapped in fog. The street lights had a
dull glow as though they were hanging in heaven.
People drifted about the streets like ghosts, the collars
of their coats drawn up to their ears.

'So this is the London I lived in for so long? How
did I endure it?'

'Tis too cold,' said Obi.

'But you grew up here.'

'I prefer it in Lagos,' the boy said. 'I can play there'.

And Liza smiled. 'Yes, that's why we went back. Your father George Nando wants to live in England forever. He's a black whiteman. But its okay for him. He is a man already, not a boy like you.'

They did not speak again until the London taxi driver said, 'Ere we are! 'Eathrow Airport.'

They handed him the precious sterling. Porters off-loaded and wheeled their baggage into the departure hall. They were already thinking of the noise and chatter of Lagos.

'Let's go upstairs and have a sandwich,' said Liza.

'Our flight is not due for another two hours at least.'

'We came too early?' asked Obi.

'It's better that way.'

Chapter Fourteen

Love Bird and Sugar Daddy

Jagua Nana's daughter received her mother and Tobias in the new place — a duplex. Judge Macros occupied one wing and Jagua's daughter the other, but the retiring Judge spent most his time with Jagua Nana's daughter.

'This place is nice,' said Jagua Nana. She looked at the soft furnishings, felt the padded chairs, gazed at herself in the large wall to wall mirror.

Tobias nodded his appreciation. From the window, they looked into the garden and saw Titi pushing Ngozi on a swing, while Obi was riding a rocking iron-horse. In the background a policeman was sitting on a swing but he had his gun over his knees and was dozing away in the humid morning air.

'My bodyguard,' said Liza.

'Na so?' Jagua said, 'Anybody wan kill you?'

'How will I know? Judge does not want any trouble. Those two men — George Nando and Saka can do anything. But I'm not worried.'

'God go protect you, Bebe Jagua.'

The steward in white served drinks.

'What next?' asked Tobias.

'You are leaving for Bendel tomorrow?' Liza asked.

'They're still surveying the land,' said Tobias. 'The place is less than fifty kilometres from Benin, just off the highway, virgin bush.' Tobias went into some detail. Traffic moving northwards from Lagos could drive in and big trailers could park. There was a petrol station, and on another side, a row of eating houses, just like in Akwanga but better.

'Yes, is like Akwanga' Jagua smiled. 'Remember?'

'Is the only business I know'· said Tobias and he gave her a knowing look.

'I am glad it is going well,' said Liza. 'What about the bank?'

'They need some few more documents, but I can find them,' Tobias said.

Jagua moved, panther-like, about the sitting room. Liza could never stop admiring her mother.

'God made you well,' she said.

'And you take after me.'

They talked about the will left behind by Nick Papadopoulous.

'Now that Auntie Kate is dead, I may have to travel to Papa's home in Greece to know the position. I am not so worried. For my part, Auntie Kate could have everything. She·was his wife.'

'And you are de daughter, or stepdaughter?'

'Real daughter with a real mother,' Liza corrected. Anyway, I'm not worried. The Judge is here and he will help in every way.'

'By de way, how do you...' Jagua said, and stopped.

'He's a good man, said Liza. 'He treats me like a goddess.' Bebe Jagua smiled.

There was a rustling in the doorway, and Judge Macros stood there. He was a big man, and seen without his robes and wig, not so intimidating.

Without his glasses he tended to squint. The grey
bush on his head needed trimming but his skin
glowed with health.

'Darling Liz,' he said.

Liza went towards him and he reached out and
held her by the bottom. An electric current passed
through her. She could feel it, and immediately
became horny. At that moment, she noticed the
pleasant glow that spread through his features and his
face shone and his eyes reflected the light on the
ceiling. He looked into her eyes with greed. He felt
twenty years younger.

'I am the luckiest man alive,' he said. Liza, playing
the pet, simply smiled. She pecked him on the cheek
and released herself. God, what was happening to
her, a man nearing his sixties, by all accounts past his
middle age, and each time he touched her she felt
aroused and charged.

'Will you have a soda?' she said.

'Yes dear. And something more, later.' Again he
slapped her on the rump.

Judge Macros sat down and crossed his legs. He
was trembling.

Tobias was all servility. 'Me Lord, Sir . . .'

'Ah, Tobias! . . . and Jagua. You two settled your
problems?'

'With the help of your wife, sir.'

The word 'Wife' sounded unusual.

'She's brilliant,' said Judge Macros. 'If there are
any problems, I'm sure she can handle them . . .
brilliant girl.'

'When do you leave for Benin?'

'Tomorrow, me lord.'

'I hope to be driving past there before the year is out. Can I look in?'

'We shall build a special V.I.P. chalet for you, me lord! said Tobias.'

'Marvellous! I could use some rest.'

Liza floated into the room, carrying a silver tray with tall glasses and sparkling soda.

'Darling when are we going to Ogabu?' Judge Macros asked.

'About Christmas time.'

'I look forward to it.'

And then it was time to go. Jagua walked towards the Judge and curtsied. 'You two live in peace'.

She extended her hand. Judge Macros took it with a gleam in his eyes. 'My mother-in-law! I don't know who is younger. Jagua Nana, or Jagua Nana's daughter.'

Tobias folded his arms behind his back and bowed.

'Well, goodbye,' said Judge Macros. 'Have a safe journey back.'

'Goodbye, me Lord, and thank you.'

Jagua and Tobias both walked down the stone steps, across the large garden and were heading towards the gate, with Liza seeing them off.

Tobias said, 'Where is Tamuno?'

'Back at school,' said Liza. 'I enrolled her for remedial studies. she says she wants to be a lawyer — like me. I'm flattered. I'll do my best for her.'

'She deserves it,' said Tobias.

'Her room is over there. She lives with us. You won't even know she's here.'

They crossed the lawn and knocked at the door. Tamuno in a light housecoat, greeted them.

'Sorry to disturb you,' said Liza, 'Mother wants to say goodbye.'

Tamuno smiled. 'Thank you.' She shook hands with Jagua Nana and Tobias.

As they walked towards the gate, Jagua turned to her daughter. 'De girl change too much. If you see her in Krinameh — eh? Like tiger. Now she done see de worl.' As for me, am glad. My son Nnochi die, and now God give me one son-in-law, one daughter and am too happy.'

Liza said nothing. She felt the tears coming. Tobias climbed into the Range Rover and it sparked to life. Slowly he eased it into the main road. Liza stood there for some time. Then she heard Judge Macros calling out to her. She recognised the love call. She moved back into the sitting room. There was a look on Judge Macros face which she understood. She moved into his arms and he edged her ever so gently into the bedroom.

When they arrived in Greece, they stayed at the Athenium Hotel. Judge Okeh Macros stripped and put on a bathing suit and went into the salty water of the lake. Liza set about locating the Papadopoulous family. Eventually she was given directions to come that evening and speak with the aged sister of her father. They lived in a splendid house off the sea coast. Liza went there with Judge Macros, and he was introduced as the husband.

'We have long connections with Nigeria,' said Nick's sister, a handsome woman with a tanned acquiline nose. You have two brothers, Paul and Stephen. Do you know them?'

Bebe Jagua's heart leapt. The tears began to steal down her cheeks.

'They live in Africa. One of them is in Construction and lives in Kenya. The other one is somewhere in Nigeria. He is running a soft drinks factory, and a motor assembly plant. Both of them are naturalised Nigerians.'

'Thank God. I thought I was alone in the world. One day I shall meet them.'

'This journey has been worth it.' Judge Macros said.

'I love you more.'

'And Auntie Kate?' Bebe Jagua asked her new-found Auntie.

She was told that the will had been executed. Auntie Kate had taken her share, but the executors had not allowed her to take more than she was due for.

'Do you want to stay here?' Liza's aunt asked.

'No, just on a visit. We have work to do at home in Africa.'

'Plenty,' said Judge Macros.

'How I wish my mother were here,' said Liza. 'Jagua Nana in Athens.'

'Bring her next time,' said Liza's Auntie.

'I will.'

'And so, we've seen my other family,' said Liza linking hands with Judge Macros.

'Great people, great indeed.'

'As soon as we get back to Nigeria we must go to Ogabu.'

'Definitely, and Badagry.'

'I'm so excited. At last, life is good.'

When they finally visited the Benin Expressway and told Tobias and Jagua Nana about all their experiences, she was happy.

She said, 'You see how God work. I born one pickin' Nnochi. He die. Now God pay me with Nene Jagua. And give me husband, this good man Tobias Momah. God's time is the best. And in-law for Greek country.'

They ate a dinner of rice with antelope meat. Construction was still going on, but from the look of things, Tobias would make out well.

'What I want to do,' said Judge Macros with a glass of red wine in his hand and the satisfaction of a well-cooked dinner below his belt, is to settle down and write my memoirs, my life story. I shall call it THE COFFIN-NAILERS, that is my story of African Judges, not all of them but my kind that bend the law to support the government.' He laughed.

After a while he seemed to remember what he had said and laughed again.

'I like you,' said Jagua Nana. 'God done give my pickin good husband. Eliza, hold am well-oh. Don' be like me, run from one man to another.'

Liza laughed.

'If she runs', said Judge Macros, 'I shall catch her,' and he suited the action to the word.

They embraced Jagua and Tobias and retired for the night.

www.ingramcontent.com/pod-product-compliance
Lightning Source LLC
Chambersburg PA
CBHW070521100726
47907CB00004B/930